DONNÉE PATRESE

I0618465

BURNED

Deadly Desires

First Draft Publishing
www.FirstDraftPublishing.com

Burned: Deadly Desires
ISBN: 978-0-9894772-8-4

For information regarding this book contact

First Draft Publishing
Info@FirstDraftPublishing.com

First Draft Publishing is a Brand of
Focus 1 Enterprises, LLC
Indianapolis, Indiana
Copyright © 2020
May 2020

Purchase of book can also be done online.

www.BurnedBook.com

Donnée Patrese

Donnée Patrese is an erotic romance and romantic suspense writer from Gary, IN. Her works include *Prohibited: an erotic novel*, *Prohibited 2: illicit affairs*, *Prohibited 3: Final Betrayal* and *Diary of a Wanted Woman*. She has two short story anthologies, *Insomnia: What happens when you can't sleep* and *Erotic Encounters*. An avid blogger and Youtuber, you can find her in her studio making videos and taking care of her husband and daughters. She has a BA in Journalism from Butler University in Indianapolis, IN and is a member of the California Writers Club. She lives in Bakersfield, CA with her family.

Love her stories and looking for a way to get better access to Donnèe and more content? Looking to get exclusive short stories and acknowledgement in one of her short story Anthologies?

Tantalizing Stories by Donnèe Patrese is on Patreon. You want to be the first to get free readings from my new books before they even launch? Well you can get that and much more. Check her out on Patreon. https://www.patreon.com/donneepatrese

Follow her on:

Instagram | https://instagram.com/Donnee_Patrese
Twitter | https://twitter.com/Donnee_Patrese
Facebook | https://www.facebook.com/DonneePatrese
Website | www.DonneePatrese.com

PROLOGUE

My fingers wrapped around her soft, delicate neck and squeezed. She struggled under my weight. I pushed harder against her throat.

"Just be quiet," I said continuing to press and tighten.

It wasn't supposed to be this way. I just wanted her. I only wanted what was mine.

"Please…" she mouthed no longer able to find her voice.

I couldn't stop. I couldn't let her go.

If she isn't mine, she doesn't deserve to be here…

It started off as a normal night. Sarah was charged with going over the evening's take in the back office. I was there as always to help anyway I could.

"The girls aren't pulling in the same amount of cash the last six months as they did last year," she said shaking her head. "I don't think it's the clients. I think some of the girls are skimming money."

I was sitting on the brown leather sofa. I was barely listening to what she was saying. Focusing on her beautiful lips as words flowed from them, I thought about what it would be like to make love to her again. It used to be wonderful between us, until she was taken away from me.

Her gorgeous red hair and small petite frame caught my eye the first time I laid eyes on her. She showed up at the club desperately looking for work. It was love at first sight.

"Are you listening to me?" she questioned. "Tony isn't going to like this."

I stood from the couch and walked over to where she sat behind a large oak desk. I closed her laptop.

"What are you doing?" she asked. "I have work to do. Tony…"

"Sarah, forget about Tony for a moment. You do too much." I moved behind her and placed my hands on her shoulders. I began to knead and massage, moving up to her neck. "All of this can wait," I said.

She didn't argue. She relaxed, accepting the rub down. A moaned escaped from her lips.

"That does feel good," she confessed.

I didn't want to let her go but I had a special treat for her.

"Let me get us a drink. That will help us loosen up."

She was hesitant.

"I should finish going over these…"

"Just one drink then you can get back to work." I negotiated.

I walked over to the wet bar in the corner and poured us both a whiskey and cola. I added something special to hers. It would be the key to getting me what I wanted.

She smiled and took the glass full of clear brown liquid from me.

She took a sip and sat the glass down on her desk.

"No, no," I said grabbing her drink and putting it back in her hand.

"Drink up. It will help you unwind."

She cocked her head to the side. Her red curls spilled down her shoulder. She grinned.

"Ok, let's do it together like old times."

I smiled back.

"Deal!"

She sat up straight and put the glass close to her lips. I copied her movements and brought my glass to my lips.

"Ready...Set...Go!" She said with a giggle.

She threw her head back and chugged the drink. I could see the muscles in her throat working. I threw my head back as well and drank as much of it as I could. I needed the liquid courage for what I was about to do.

She slammed the empty tumbler down on the desk. I laughed at the look on her face.

"What was in that? It tasted terrible."

I chuckled.

"It did have a funky after taste," I said. "Maybe that cola I used was flat."

She shook her head furiously.

"Yuck," she exclaimed.

I laughed again.

"Okay, breaks over," she insisted. "Now I really need to get back to work."

She reopened her laptop. I sat in the chair across from the desk and stared at her. I watched until I knew the drugs I'd given her kicked in.

There was enough Xanax crushed up in her drink to knock out a 200lb man.

It was easy to see when they began to course through her veins and take effect on her body and mind. She tried to stand but fell back down in her chair.

"I feel," she began "I don't feel well. I think I drank that too fast."

I stood and grabbed her by the arms. I led her over to the brown leather couch.

"Lay down," I said. "Maybe resting will make you feel better."

I left for a moment to lock the door. She tried to sit up but the drugs were too much. She lay there not moving. Moans escaped from her mouth. The sounds she made turned me on. I leaned over her and began to caress her small breasts through her green dress. She groaned fueling my desire.

My hand slid up her pale freckled thighs until they found her panties. My fingers moved the material out the way. I found and began to play with her clit. She was surprisingly wet and I continued to rub her.

I knew I turned her on...

Suddenly her groans turned into actual words. She began to plead.

"No, please, no."

She reached down with slow movements trying to pull her dress down. I ignored her plea and continued my exploration. My fingers worked in and out of her. I pulled them out and licked her juices from each one before placing two of them back inside.

She began to struggle more and more. She squirmed and kicked at me. I was surprised. The medication should have knocked her out by now. I knew I should have given her more but I was afraid. But, too much would have killed her.

What am I going to do?

"Stop," she demanded.

Her struggles became more powerful. I decided to straddle and pin her down with my weight. My body pressed against hers only made me more aroused.

"No!" she screamed.

The volume of her voice caused me to jump. I didn't think she had enough strength. She followed it up with more yelling.

"Help me!" she shouted.

I had to shut her up.

We weren't the only ones in the lounge and I knew eventually someone would hear us. I placed my hand over her mouth.

"Shut up Sarah," I whispered.

She didn't listen. Muffled screams escaped. Panic and arousal set in for me. It was strange. I needed her to be quiet but the fight in her was so stimulating.

But…I couldn't have her screaming.

She needs to be quiet.

Before I knew it, my fingers were around her neck and I was trying hard to keep her from shrieking. She clawed at my face and hands. I continued to compress her windpipe. She wanted to free herself. I couldn't let that happen.

I could feel my desire increase as she fought for her life. I held her existence in my hands and there was nothing she could do about it. Her struggles excited me. I felt so exhilarated having that kind of power.

If she didn't want me, no one could have her.

That thought flowed through my mind as her hazel eyes began to bulge and her attempts at freedom became weaker and weaker. She pulled at my fingers until she couldn't resist anymore. The medication and the lack of oxygen won over. It turned me on to feel her between my thighs.

Her eyes closed and I felt her body go limp. I needed to be safe so I continued to apply pressure until I was too exhausted to go on. I took two fingers and pressed them firmly against her neck.

No pulse.

I checked again.

She was dead.

Sarah had passed away.

I   killed   her…and   it   felt   invigorating!

CHAPTER 1

Kimberly

"Where were you when the body was found?" the detective asked me.

I was in a state of fear and shock. My mind was blank and I couldn't remember anything. I searched my brain for something to tell him but I couldn't. I ended up giving him a blank stare.

The entire lounge was in turmoil. Half-naked women were crying in the arms of bouncers and police officers. Some were being questioned about their whereabouts when the tragedy took place. The hysterical ones were being treated by EMTs.

The anarchy was making it very difficult for me to think or completely process what was happening. The dead body in the back room didn't make things any easier.

"Miss," the detective said looking down at his notebook and then back at me. "Lawson. Miss Lawson, where were you when Sarah Ludamine's body was found?"

He waited for my answer and prepared to write down whatever came out of my mouth.

I searched my mind for something, anything to say. This was information I should know.

I couldn't remember a damn thing.

"I'm not sure,"

He went to write down what I said then stopped. I'm assuming I didn't answer the question to his satisfaction because he put down his notepad and pen, then folded his arms across his chest. He raised an eyebrow.

"You don't know where you were?"

I could feel sweat drip down the nape of my neck. I had never been questioned by the police before. My chest was tight and my body shook. It was a wonder I could remember my name.

"I mean, I think I was at the bar…I don't know."

At that moment, a few police officers and the medical examiner pushed the body from the back room on a stretcher. It was completely enclosed in a plastic black zippered sleeping bag type thing. That was enough to send the room erupting into chaos. There were wails and shrieks coming from all around,

As they took her past the bar and out through the opened front doors, I began to freak out. My heart raced and I struggled to breathe.

"Miss Lawson, FOCUS!" the detective gruffly ordered.

I turned back to face him. This guy made me nervous. He looked like one of those TV crime drama detectives. He was pale with shoulder length dark brown hair. He was wearing a black trench coat over a brown suit. I began to wring my hands hoping this would be over soon.

"Okay, try answering this question. How well did you know the victim?"

I didn't have to think hard about the answer. It was my first day on the job, I barely knew anyone except April.

April was an old friend of my mom's from high school. She and my mom were very close and they kept in touch even when distance kept them apart. My parents knew she lived close to where I planned to attend college, so they asked her to take in their scholarship-deprived daughter.

April was cool with letting me live with her as long as I stayed in school, held down a job, and donated to the finances. I didn't think that was a difficult thing to do until it took me forever to find work. I would have asked April to put me on with her but from the beginning I knew she didn't have an ordinary occupation. She worked only nights and was paid in cash. Her place was full of expensive furniture and her jewelry collection was ridiculous.

She worked at a lounge called *Inferno*. The rumors swirling around the college campus about that place were explicit. They said it was a modern day brothel and the women that worked there were being paid for sex. April insisted she was a hostess and nothing like that was going on at the lounge. I had my suspicions. Yet, I was too afraid to press her. How do you insist to someone they were prostituting? Eventually she confessed. She was a "companion" and yes…she was paid to have sex.

April offered to put in a good word for me at the lounge. I declined. Once I found out what she did, I felt sorry for her. I always felt any woman working in the sex industry had no self respect and plenty of daddy issues. I told April that. She was insulted and proud of what she did for a living.

Six months after not finding a job and no money in my pocket, I began to rethink her offer…

"I didn't know Sarah very well," I replied. "I just started working here."

He tilted his head to the side and again raised an eyebrow.

"Tell me Miss Lawson, what exactly do you do here?"

My eyes widened and my mind raced. I had no clue how to answer that question to a cop. It was a good thing our conversation was interrupted by a tall man with chocolate colored skin. He was gorgeous in a navy blue polo shirt and black slacks. His classically handsome features left me speechless.

"Detective, I'm Attorney Kenneth Johnson and I'll be representing Miss…"

His eye trained on me and I realized he didn't know my name.

"L…L…Lawson," I stammered.

If my mind wasn't jumbled before it would have been after I saw him. He had an aura of strength, confidence with a velvety swagger.

"Yes, I'll be representing Miss Lawson, Detective…" he said extending his hand.

"Detective Lucas Marshall," he answered taking the attorney's hand and shaking it cautiously.

My "attorney," whom I had never met before in my life, placed his hand on my back.

"Detective Marshall, Miss Lawson is my client and you have been questioning her without her attorney present. I am here to put an end to that."

Detective Marshall folded his arms across his chest.

"Miss Lawson didn't ask for an attorney and not once did she mention she had one."

The hand on my back pushed a little. I wasn't sure what he was doing. I just sat there in a daze as the two men went back and forth.

"Well, now you know she has one, there will be no more questions."

The detective completely ignored him.

"It was just a simple question. Miss Lawson what do you do here at *Inferno*?"

His eyes pierced mine and stared at me intently.

I knew at that moment, he wanted more than just information about the death of the young woman. He realized I was new and wanted me to snitch. He probably already had an investigation into this place and wanted a witness or a mole.

"Don't answer that!" Mr. Johnson ordered.

I didn't say a word. I just continued to wring my hands. I knew snitches had a short life expectancy.

"Surely she can tell me what she saw and where she was?"

"No, she cannot."

The attorney grabbed my arm and pulled me off the bar stool. He tucked me into his arms and everything else that was said was muffled by my heart pounding in my ears. Having body against mine gave me butterflies. It had been awhile since a man made me feel that way.

"Come with me," I heard him say. I followed him away from the bar. When we were far enough away from the detective, I looked up at him.

"Thank you, Mr. Johnson." I said.

He smiled.

"Call me Kenneth, Miss Lawson."

I smiled back.

"Call me Kim."

Suddenly we were approached by another man. He looked like a shorter version of the man holding on to me.

"Excuse me but I need to speak with him for a moment," he said grabbing Kenneth by the arm and pulling him away.

I was left standing alone in the middle of the mess. I looked around and realized everyone was still panicking. The body was gone but the fact that there were still police here asking questions, made the women and staff uneasy.

I sat down in a chair only to be startled by someone calling my name.

"Kim!" I heard. "Let's get the fuck out of here."

I stood and looked behind me. There was April marching across the room in my direction. She looked sad, pissed and determined all at the same time. She threw my bag at me.

"We need to get out of here and get home. I can't take being here anymore."

I reached out and grabbed her.

"Whoa, hold up. The police aren't letting anyone leave."

She placed a hand on her hip.

"Do I look like I care? The police are not guarding the bathroom window. Some of the girls have already snuck out. Let's go."

I followed without another word.

CHAPTER 2

Kenneth

She was dangerous.

Her 5'1" frame with large breasts and a thin waist drove me wild. She always wore a wig with jet black hair cut into a short bob. It contrasted nicely against her caramel complexion and dark brown eyes.

Those cocoa-colored orbs looked up at me occasionally as she sucked my dick. I knew I should stay away but my brain never seemed to work properly when I came here. *Inferno Lounge* was a weakness of mine. The beautiful women serving drinks and giving private services in the back rooms kept me coming back for more.

My older brother insisted I stay away from this place. He wanted my focus on work and settling down with a good woman. Starting a family. But how could I stay away from Wendy? Like I said, she was dangerous and had me coming harder than I ever come before.

The slurping noises Wendy made turned me on. I raised my hand and placed it on the back of her head. She bobbed up and down while I threw my head back and closed my eyes. I imagined it wasn't Wendy sucking me off. I imagined it was someone special. Someone I actually cared about. Unbeknownst to my brother, I did crave something more. I wanted a wife and a family but that never happened when I went on my search for "the one." I ended up falling for a woman already taken or a stripper that only wanted me as long as I continued to put money in her g-string.

So for now, I'll just stick to this bomb ass head and call it a day.

Her hand stroked my dick up and down the shaft. I moaned pushing her head further down. She reached up and removed my hand.

"Are you trying to choke me?" she questioned wiping saliva from her mouth.

I shook my head.

"No, but f you stop again I'm not paying you shit."

She rolled her eyes but went back to stroking and sucking getting me closer and closer.

"Oh shit," I groaned.

That is when the screaming began.

"What the fuck…" I said scrambling from the bed putting on my clothes. Wendy didn't seem bothered by the noise.

"Some bitch is always screaming around here. Maybe the dick was that good…"

But it was more than just good dick. I soon found that out when I ventured downstairs and saw the chaos.

Before I knew it the place was flooded with police. The club owner, Tony, was pulling me and my brother, Malcolm, in a corner. I wasn't sure when Malcolm arrived but when Tony called he usually came running.

"Look, I need you two to go out there and make sure no one opens their mouth," he ordered.

Malcolm, a very high profile defense attorney and the main attorney representing the lounge and its owners, protested.

"Kenneth doesn't work for you and I don't need him involved in this mess," he argued.

Malcolm turned and glared at me.

He was angry I was there at all. I promised him I would stay away, yet I was stopping by when he wasn't around seeing Wendy. I looked away trying not to catch his eye. I refrained from calling him a hypocrite. He lectured me about being at the club, when he was here all the time representing them in their affairs.

"I don't need him to actually defend anyone," Tony said. "I just need the cops to know there are lawyers around so they won't try and bully my people."

Malcolm pulled me away from Tony but not before he made his opinion known.

"No. Kenneth stays out of it. I bought along a few colleagues of mine. We can handle this…without my brother."

He then turned his attention to me.

"Because you were here when Sarah was found you can't leave…"

"I know that. I didn't go to law school for nothing," I replied.

"Good. Now take your law degree and have a seat until this is over."

"Malcolm you should just let me help."

He heaved a sigh.

"No," he answered. "Stay put."

Then he walked away heading for a group of cops questioning some of the women.

I reluctantly sat down on one of the sofas and glanced around at the scene. I noticed no one was doing a good job keeping things in order. Women were arguing, crying and fighting. I could tell some women had left. The police were already bungling this case. We lived in a large urban city. Murders were a dime a dozen. The investigations should come easy to them. Yet I knew men in a room full of half naked women could be easily distracted.

I was done with sitting. I needed to do something. I began to walk around listening to conversations between the women and the police. I stopped when I noticed one woman sitting at the bar with a detective I had never seen before. Now, as a public defender, I've met practically every detective there was to meet in the 26th precinct. This guy, never seemed to cross my path.

I looked at the woman and sensed a lot of distress. Most of the girls showed signs of anguish, but she looked like a scared fragile child. She was young, I could tell. The baby fat on her cheeks gave it away. She was wringing her hands and her eyes darted around the room as if she were looking for a way out.

I decided to walk over and listen closer to the conversation.

"What is it exactly that you do here, Miss Lawson?" I overheard the detective ask.

I knew this was the moment I needed to interrupt.

"Detective, I'm Attorney Kenneth Johnson and I'll be representing Miss..."

I looked at her and pleaded with my eyes for some help. Her eyes grew wide with understanding and I could sense some of her fears fade.

"L...L...Lawson," she stuttered.

"Yes, I'll be representing Miss Lawson, Detective..." I said extending my hand.

The detective looked at her and then at me.

"Detective Lucas Marshall," he answered taking my hand and shaking it.

"Detective Marshall, Miss Lawson is my client and I see you have been questioning her without her attorney present. I am here to put an end to that."

He folded his arms across his chest.

"Miss Lawson didn't ask for an attorney and not once did she mention she had one."

"Well, now that you know she has one, there will be no more questions."

I put my hand on her back and encouraged her to stand. Marshall was being pushy. I needed to get her away from him as soon as possible. I pushed her again but she didn't move. She froze. I could understand. She didn't know me and the trauma of the evening would leave anyone stunned.

Detective Marshall tried to use her vulnerability to his advantage.

"It was just a simple question. Miss Lawson what do you do here at *Inferno*?"

"Don't answer that!" I exclaimed.

She jumped at the sound of my voice. I looked down at her. She looked like a frightened puppy. A beautiful frightened little puppy.

"Surely she can tell me what she saw and where she was?"

I sighed. He wasn't giving up and my patience was very thin at 3 am.

"No, she cannot," I replied.

I grabbed her by the arm and literally pulled her off the barstool into my arms.

"Come with me," I said to her.

Leaving the detective pissed, I pulled her away. Suddenly she stopped and turned to me.

"Thank you, Mr. Johnson." she said.

I smiled realizing her dark brown eyes were glowing. It was at that second I realized how breath taking she was. She smiled back at me.

"Call me Kenneth, Miss Lawson," I replied.

"Call me Kim."

We stood for a second just looking at each other. I was so caught up in her beauty I didn't notice Malcolm approaching.

"Excuse me but I need to speak with him for a moment," he said grabbing me by the arm and pulling me to the side.

"What do you think you're doing? I told you to stay out of this!" Malcolm screamed.

His brow was wrinkled and his nostrils flared.

I sighed.

"Look, there was a nosy detective asking one of the girls what she did here. I didn't think Tony would appreciate that line of questioning."

He calmed down a bit releasing a long stream of air from his nose.

"Fine. But you're done here. No more helping. This is my client and I got this."

He walked away and then suddenly stopped and returned to me.

"Ken, I've seen that look in your eyes before."

"What look?" I asked confused.

He shook his head and laughed.

"There is a reason I told you to stay away. You always fall for the wrong type of girl. Don't let pussy get you caught up again."

"Malcolm, I'm fine."

He looked over my shoulder. "She is a beauty. I can see why you were so willing to swoop in and save her."

I shook my head and smiled. He reached out and patted me on the shoulder. His eyes switched from amusement to concern. "Stay away from this place, little brother," he warned before he left me alone again rushing over to stop a police officer from questioning a bouncer.

CHAPTER 3

Malcolm

"This is bullshit. Every second this place stays closed, I lose money." Tony said sitting behind his desk throwing darts at a dartboard in his lavish office. He spent more money in this room than anywhere else in the club.

The collection of paintings, the samurai swords on the wall and the large cherry wood desk had to cost more than my house. Tony knew how to spend money. Saving for a rainy day was not in his vocabulary. No wonder having the lounge closed was pissing him off.

We were all there Tony, Me, Luciano, the bouncers Jake and Jimmy, and Tony's personal bodyguards, Sugar and Skeet. We were trying to figure out what to do about Sarah's death. After the police were called to the lounge, we had to shut down all services except those reserved for the regulars. We set up the girls in hotels so they could still see their clients while we waited for *Inferno* to no longer be a crime scene.

After the murder, some of the girls quit. They were afraid this would happen again and they didn't want to put themselves in danger. Tony tried to intimidate them to see things his way but that didn't work. They said 'fuck you' and disappeared.

The incident with Sarah was unique. We've had a couple of girls overdose but that was the extent of our past troubles. The lounge wasn't considered a crime scene when those girls died and everything would go back to business as usual. After those incidences, Tony added a few more officers to his payroll and we felt secure in our protection. We even hired more security. That's why everyone was perplexed someone could kill Sarah and get away. I am convinced whoever killed her was still in the building when the police arrived. Essentially, the killer was one of us.

"Look, Tony." I said checking email on my phone. "I made a few calls to the cops we have on payroll. They said it may take a couple more days. They are still gathering evidence."

He stood, smacking items off his desk. He kicked the garbage can sending trash flying to the other side of the room.

No one flinched. We were used to his temper.

"Can you do some legal maneuvers or spout some legal mumbo-jumbo to make this go away? I can't wait much longer." Tony said.

I sighed.

Anthony Santino Jr. was the most impatient man I had ever met. He's like a child throwing tantrums all the time. My job was not only to keep him calm but to also keep an eye on him. I was hired by his father Anthony Santino Sr. He was afraid his son was going to destroy his lounge, kill someone or end up in jail.

I've been doing my best but it has been pretty rough. I mean, my job title didn't include babysitting a grown ass man. I took the job because his father gave me a huge salary, ai had practically grown up with Tony and access to all the girls at the lounge.

"When I find out who the fuck is killing bitches in my club costing me money, I'm going to kill him myself."

I sighed.

"Sitting around like this is bullshit," Jake said leaning against the wall behind Tony's chair.

I don't like Jake or Jimmy. They were the two worst security officers in history. Both were terrible at their jobs. Jake spent more time fucking girls then breaking up fights. I told Tony to find someone else but they are his childhood friends and the only people he trusts. I don't think he realized what it took to run a successful business. That was more his father's forte. He didn't understand that if you didn't invest in the things you needed you were just wasting your time. Now, it just looks like a clubhouse for little boys. If he had hired better people...Sarah might still be here.

"Shut the fuck up," Tony yelled at him. "You're already on the fucking hot seat."

Jake huffed and looked over at the club manager.

"Why am I on the hot seat? Luciano is the one in charge of the girls. Why isn't he in some kind of trouble?"

At that moment all eyes turned to Luciano. He hadn't said a word the entire meeting. He just stood staring out the window. Tony and I knew how distraught he was over losing Sarah. He had a special bond with all the girls. I didn't like Jake trying to throw him under the bus.

"Jake, shut the fuck up," I said. "You're fucking security. You or Jimmy had to be the one that let the mother fucker in." I said shaking my head.

His face was red now. I knew he was angry. I didn't give a fuck. He's 6'5" and 375 lbs of pussy. He wouldn't make a move if his life depended on it.

"Well, what about you Mr. Big Shot attorney?"

I raised an eyebrow.

"What about me?"

He came toward me and I stood. If he wanted a fight I would give him one.

"Are you doing your fucking job? Are you fixing this shit? Are you earning all the money you're being paid?"

I laughed and sat back down in my chair.

"You are more ignorant than I thought. I'm not getting paid enough to clean up the mess you've made."

"Please," he said "You're too busy fucking these bitches to look out for Tony's best interest. I wonder what your wife would think if she knew about that."

That was the last straw. No one talked about my wife. Tony knew that too and got up and stood between us.

"Jake, shut up and go back over there. If you say anymore smart ass shit to Malcolm, I am going to make Sugar and Skeet hold you down while he kicks the fuck out of you."

Jake walked away but I knew this wasn't the end. I was going to have to kick his ass.

"Look, Malcolm and I need to talk. The rest of you get the fuck out."

They all started to file out talking amongst themselves. When they were gone, Tony pulled out a blunt, lit it up and started to smoke it.

He took a puff and then offered it to me. I turned it down and he shook his head. He took another puff blowing the smoke across the room.

"The motherfucker is dead. When I find out who this cock sucker is, I am going to fucking gut him."

Tony was always making threats. He threatened to kill everybody. He was like the Red Queen from Alice and Wonderland. "Off with their heads." If anything ever happened however, Tony wouldn't do it. It would be done by his enforcer Sugar or someone else loyal to his father.

However, this time I truly believed him. I believed that if he found out who killed Sarah...Let's just say, I felt sorry for the guy.

Tony's married with three kids. He told me all the time he cared about his wife but he only married her because she got knocked up. His family would have disowned him if he hadn't. His dad's very traditional.

So while working in his lounge, he began to have sex with as many women as he could. I believed it was his way of trying to find the love he was missing. I knew he would do anything for his wife, but they slept in separate bedrooms. I don't think they have had much sex since their last child was born seven years ago.

When Sarah started working at *Inferno*, she became the only girl he made love to. He would do anything she wanted. She had him by the balls and pretty soon she became his mistress. She was the queen of the club. Even Ashley, a self-proclaimed "baddest bitch" bowed down to her.

He spent more time with her than he spent at home. He bought her a house, a car, and her entire wardrobe. I listened to him rant about money and how much of it he was losing but I knew it was more about Sarah. He was supposed to be tough so he couldn't cry about losing her. It could be very difficult not being able to fully mourn the woman you loved.

I wanted to stay, smoke a blunt and help him mourn, but I didn't think he was in a mood to talk to anyone coherently right now. He was in too much pain. It didn't matter; I had an important appointment to keep anyway. I was meeting my brother Kenneth for lunch and I had a few choice words to say to him. I was pissed. I have told him repeatedly not to show up at the club, especially without telling me. It wasn't until after all the chaos started and Sarah was discovered dead, I learned my brother was amongst the mayhem. When I found out…there was almost two murders.

"Malcolm, how was I supposed to know that a girl was going to die?" Kenneth said.

I could have kicked his ass. I would have if there weren't so many police around.

I brought my attention back to Tony and noticed he was still ranting about what he would do if he caught the guy who killed Sarah.

"Tony," I said interrupting his rant. "As long as the girls are making money out of the hotel you're still getting paid. Plus, they are not investigating you. The cops you are so handsomely bribing are making sure the attention stays off you and the girls. The cops actually want to know who killed Sarah."

"I'm still losing money Malcolm."

"Well, have you talked to your father? He is going to need to be in on this."

"Malcolm, I don't want my father involved at all."

I knew he was going to say that. However, Antonio Sr. was the one that technically owned the lounge. He gave it to his son but according to the paperwork Senior still owned it.

"Fine, but he is going to probably get involved sooner or later."

He just continued to smoke his blunt.

"Malcolm, figure out how to get this shit straightened out. Just do your job!"

I stood and looked at him.

"I am going to let you get away with that bullshit this time because I know this isn't just about money. I know you're hurting and you are taking it out on me. I know you loved Sarah. So grieve and I will keep you posted on what is going on with the club. I'll handle those losers out there and that should give you time."

He looked up at me and sighed.

"My heart is broken, Malcolm."

"I know. We'll get this taken care of. But look, I have a very important meeting to attend. If you need to, give me a call." I said.

"Whatever," he said taking another puff of his blunt.

CHAPTER 4

Kimberly

"Oh baby," I groaned as Luciano's tongue played with my clit.

My moans filled the room and my juices filled his mouth. I focused on the pleasure and not on the man. It made it easier to do what I did. I had only been working at *Inferno Lounge* a couple of weeks and I was already considered pretty lucky.

My only client has been the lounge manager Luciano Valentino. Most of the girls were swamped with clients. They were all trying to make up for the loss of money during the shutdown of the lounge and subsequent investigation into the death of Sarah.

I don't think I would consider myself lucky, however. When I first met Luciano, the last thing I would have thought I would be doing was sleeping with him. He seemed creepy and not what I would have considered attractive. He was 35 years older than me at 54. Not to mention he was short, plump and balding.

His strength was in his kindness and generosity. He was gentle and very affectionate with all the girls. He treated us like we were special and he genuinely cared about our welfare. He was a breath of fresh air from all the men I saw treating the women like property.

That affection was something we needed more than anything. Most of the girls were terrified and saddened by the death of Sarah. It was harder now for some of the women to be alone with new clients or as they were called in the lounge a "clean consumer."

It was one of the reasons I was considered fortunate. My only client was Luciano and everyone trusted him. Plus, he rarely wanted sex. Well, he wanted sex he just couldn't produce. Complications with diabetes left him impotent and because of a heart condition, drugs that typically treat Erectile Dysfunction were off limits to him. He finally accepted his fate and dedicated his time to pleasuring women. Right now, I was the meal of the day.

"Right there. Please don't stop," I groaned.

My toes curled feeling electricity running through them. My orgasm moved from my clit to the rest of my body. It spread like fire through my veins.

"Oh," I moaned making sure to keep my eyes closed.

He continued to eat my pussy and I pretended he was someone else.

My body convulsed. I pressed my body up and down until finally exhausted, I collapsed onto the bed. My breathing was labored as I rode the final wave of my orgasm.

"That seemed like a good one." Luciano said wiping my juices from his mouth with the back of his hand.

I smiled and sat up on my elbows.

"That was amazing. You are the best." I said reaching down to caress his head.

He moved up on the bed and pulled me into his arms. He tried to kiss me. I moved my head back. He moved with me and was successful in kissing me on the lips.

When he pulled back I laid on his hairy chest. I could hear his heart beating.

"Kim," he began. "You make me feel so good. I want to please you and give you whatever you want." He paused for a second then continued. "I would love you like no one else," he confessed.

I chuckled awkwardly. April told me not to get attached to any client. Most importantly you couldn't let them get too attached to you. You wanted to please them just enough to keep them coming back but not enough that they wanted to leave their wives for you or make you their wife. It's only been a couple of weeks and Luciano was already trying to do just that.

I decided it was time for me to leave.

"Luciano, you're so sweet," I said sitting up. "I don't need you to give me the world. I'll just settle for my payment."

He laughed then reached over onto the side table next to the bed and grabbed his wallet. He opened it, looked at me, then closed it back.

"Why don't we just cuddle for awhile? I'll pay you double," he said stroking my arm.

I climbed off the bed and began putting on my clothes.

"Sorry, I really need to go. We can cuddle some other time."

He looked disappointed. He opened his wallet and pulled out some bills then handed them to me. I leaned down and kissed him on the cheek.

"I'll come back and see you when my shift is over," I promised him.

I escaped the room and decided I needed to clean up before I went looking for April. After my shower, I dressed and headed downstairs. I saw April at the bar laughing and talking with the bartender Sasha.

I remember the day I met Sasha. I had come into the lounge looking for a job. I was nervous, dejected and upset I had made the choice to be a "companion." It took a lot of soul searching. I found I was devoted to my education and I would do anything to graduate from college. I had no money and felt I had no choice. I had to do this for my parents. I was their only child and they lived to see me get my degree. So I made the ultimate decision...

The first time I walked into the lounge I was shocked. I expected to see a bar, dance floor, tables, everything you would see in a normal after hours spot. However, the inside looked more like someone's living room. It was tasteful and very beautiful. There was a bar where you could get drinks but it had the atmosphere of a calm sexual house party.

When I arrived, I was greeted by Sasha.

"We're closed," she said wiping off some drink glasses.

"I know you're closed, I'm here to meet with Mr. Valentino."

She laughed.

"What's so funny?" I asked confused.

She shook her head.

"Wait right there."

As she walked from around the bar my eyes stayed glued to her. Her entire body was covered in tattoos. Her long hair had rainbow colored tips and her skin was the color of the ebony keys on a piano. The contrast of colors was fascinating.

She stopped suddenly and turned to look at me. I guess she could feel my eyes on her because she smiled.

"Just so you know cutie, don't stare unless you want some."

That memory plays in my head every time I see Sasha.

When April saw me approach, she began to clap.

"Uh Oh, Kim is legit. She's been on the job for two weeks now."

I rolled my eyes and smiled.

"Not sure if you can call her legit," Sasha said wiping off the counter. "She's only been with Luciano. I don't believe that counts."

I knew she was referring to the fact he was impotent. I opened my mouth to reply but April chimed in for me.

"Leave her alone. She's putting out and getting paid. That's legit in my book. Plus," she said slapping me on the back as I occupied the stool next to her. "She'll be branching out in no time. I'm sure once word gets out about Kim, there will be a line around the block for her."

My eyes grew wide at the thought. Sasha noticed and laughed.

"Here," she said taking a shot glass full of a clear fluid and slid it over to me. "I think you might need that."

I grabbed the glass and downed it quickly.

"Whoa!" I said. My throat and chest burned as the strong liquid went down.

I knew taking this job meant that I would be having sex with men I didn't know but now being confronted with the realization that it was really going to happen terrified me.

I was happy when someone else caught April's and Sasha's attention. A young light-skinned woman with long dark curly hair walked by us heading upstairs toward the VIP rooms. She barely looked where she was going. All of her attention was dedicated to whatever was on her cell phone.

"Hey Abigail!" April called out to her.

The woman just waved her hand at April never taking her eyes from her phone. Once she was out of sight…the gossiping started.

"I'm surprised she's here. I wouldn't have come back after seeing something like that." April said leaning across the bar to Sasha.

I agreed with April. I had no idea how Abigail could come back to this place like nothing happened. Abigail was the one that found Sarah dead. Apparently they were close and she went looking for her at the end of her shift. She found Sarah deceased on the couch in the back office.

"I heard Tony threatened holy hell if she didn't come back," Sasha replied.

"I would have said…" April throws up her index and middle finger. "PEACE!" she said before they both laughed.

I wasn't sure how they could find anything funny about a dead girl and her friend finding her. I felt bad for Abigail. That had to be traumatic. Something like that could change a person.

While they sat laughing and gossiping some more, we were approached by a woman about 5'2", with a caramel complexion and shoulder length jet black hair. Her name was Wendy and she was one of the original women at the lounge. When *Inferno Lounge* opened, she was my age. After 16 years, companionship became a career. She was atop the hierarchy and according to April, her clients were her clients and they were not to be messed with.

Occupying the bar stool next to April, Wendy began to play a guessing game.

"Guess what?" she asked.

April and Sasha looked at each other. Sasha rolled her eyes.

"I'll play," I replied. "What's going on?"

Wendy shot a glance at me. She raised an eyebrow and flared her nostrils. I could tell she was appalled I had the nerve to talk to her directly. She promptly ignored me.

"Someone's back from Hawaii," she said.

I had no clue who could be coming back from Hawaii. April and Sasha exchanged looks again. April's eyes were as big as saucers and Sasha's eyes were filled with dread. I remembered April telling me there was one other woman that had higher ranking than Wendy. I had never met her but it looked like that was going to change.

A tall buxom woman approached. She was wearing an extremely short skirt and a shirt that looked more like lingerie. Her ass and breasts were enormous and I could tell that none of it came naturally. Not even the long dark brown hair that draped down to her butt. Wendy stood and the woman occupied her spot.

April turned to face her.

"Hi, Ashley," she said through gritted teeth. "You look rested and less bitchy." The sarcasm was rich in her tone.

"My three week vacation in Hawaii was amazing," Ashley replied. "I'm kind of sad I had to come back to you bitches."

"I stand corrected," April said sticking out her tongue.

I giggled.

For the first time Ashley realized I was there. I could tell she was not happy to see me. She stood and made her way over. She looked me up and down.

"Who is this cutie with the box braids?" she asked to no one in particular.

"She's the new girl I was telling you about," Wendy replied. "April brought her on."

"Well, I would like to know what's so funny," she said taking a step closer to me.

I was not one to be intimidated. April said my mouth was going to get me in trouble. I guess today was going to be that day.

"You wouldn't understand," I responded standing. "It's an inside joke and you're just not on the inside."

I smiled placing my hand on my hip. I felt cocky and strong. I planned to treat this like a prison. Find the baddest bitch and take her down. The looks on April and Sasha's faces told me they didn't agree with my tactic and as Ashley moved in on me April jumped in between us.

"Ashley, I'm sure you have a client waiting,"

Ashley glared at me.

"You're right April I do. That is the only thing saving her from an ass whooping. In the meantime, April, you need to rein in your mini-me. Make sure she knows the rules. I'm the Queen bitch and what's mine is mine. No one fucks with my clients."

"Or mine," Wendy added.

They headed upstairs like they owned the place.

I knew at that moment those girls were going to be a problem.

"I'm out," I said to April and Sasha and walked away as well.

I was exhausted. Good thing my shift was almost over. I had been here all evening and that was after a full day of classes. Once I got home I had some studying to do. I was supposed to be here another 40 minutes. Causing enough drama for the day, I decided to hide out in Luciano's office.

He was at his desk when I walked in eyes glued to his laptop.

"What are you busy doing?" I asked making my way over to his nice comfy brown couch.

He smiled at me.

"Just payroll. Sarah used to be in charge of that…"

He sighed.

I was done thinking or talking about Sarah's demise. I didn't know her, but her death consumed me. It was so sad and I was reminded of it every day that I came. *Would I get the client that ended her life? Who was he?*

I walked over to him and set some money on his desk. Even though Luciano was my only client I had to still give the club their 25%.

He looked at the money and picked it up. He handed it back to me.

"Keep it baby."

I looked at him confused.

"This is the lounge's cut." I said.

"Keep it. I'll pay your percentage," he said.

I smiled and kissed him on top of his balding head.

Walking over to the couch, I laid across it.

"Could you wake me up when you're done?" I asked closing my eyes.

I was so tired. I just wanted 20 minutes of sleep.

"Sweetie, you look beat," he said.

I opened my eyes.

"It's been a long day," I said rubbing my fingers across my eyes. "I met the queen bitch."

He laughed.

CHAPTER 5

Malcolm

Ashley was good at her job. I had been a recipient of her magic for the past three years. I watched her as she stroked my dick and drew circles around the head with her tongue. She was on her knees in front of me. Her large breasts lay firmly against the edge of the couch.

On most evenings when I was alone with Ashley, my wife would be the furthest thing from my mind. Yet tonight…she was front and center in my thoughts, making it difficult to stay hard while Ashley serviced me.

I had been married for ten years and the last four have been passionless and boring. She just didn't do it sexually for me anymore and if I'm honest, our connection had been lost. Between me working all the time and she not keeping herself up, it was bound to happen

Don't get me wrong. My wife, Evelyn, is an amazing woman. She's smart, talented, a full time writer and an incredible mother to our two young children. I just didn't look at her anymore and wanted to bend her over and fuck her senseless like I did Ashley.

I love my wife and would do anything for her…except be faithful. That I could not do. A man has needed and when I need them met, I came down to *Inferno*. I hang out, have a few drinks then take Ashley upstairs to the VIP rooms and have my way with her.

No matter what, I still came home to my wife. None of that meant I had any plans to leave. We have a beautiful little girl and a handsome son together. Neither of us would do anything to disrupt their lives. I may not be faithful but I am committed.

My emotions were never involved when I fucked Ashley. That's just not how this worked. Unlike, my emotional brother Kenneth. He fell for every stripper or whore that showed him a little too much attention. My goal was to never fall for one of these women. It was one of the many reasons I only messed around with Ashley.

She knew my rules about discretion and she did a good job making sure it's just sex and nothing more. She didn't try to make me her sugar daddy and she didn't do something stupid like fall for me. She's been in the game long enough to know I would drop her quick if she tried that mess. I'm not Tony. The last thing I needed was a mistress.

The problem with being with the same escort for so long was the same reason I got so bored with my wife. She's pretty much done all the tricks in her arsenal and probably some of them three or four times.

Tonight I just wasn't feeling her.

I could tell she noticed my lack of enthusiasm.

"What's going on in that head of yours, Malcolm?" she asked.

Here I was sitting on a couch butt ass naked with a beautiful woman on her knees giving me head and I was struggling to keep hard.

"I'm thinking this is probably not going to work out tonight. I have too much on my mind,"

She sat back on her heels.

"Just give me a few more minutes. I can make you forget all about your problems."

Yesterday, that may have worked. Tonight, I didn't think I was going to get hard for anyone.

"No, Ashley. I think I need to head home. It's getting late."

I stood from the couch and began to redress.

"Well, I serviced you. Just because you can't get hard doesn't mean I don't get paid."

I laughed. Good girl…she's all business.

I pulled my wallet from my pants pocket and slid out a few hundred dollars. I handed the bills over to her. She grabbed them and stood.

"I have clients all day tomorrow. You have to find another day to get at me," she added.

I buttoned my shirt then stuffed it into my pants.

"I guess I'll have to find someone else to fuck."

She pulled on her robe and tied it around her waist.

"It better not be a bitch from here," she said one hand on her hip.

I laughed.

I finished tying my tie and grabbed my jacket.

"Goodnight Ashley." I said as I left the room.

I headed downstairs away from the VIP rooms and into the lounge. The atmosphere was calm and laid back. It was the vibe that Tony wanted. He liked a place that was sensual and classy. He refused, against his father's wishes, to open a wild club or a strip joint.

I decided once I entered the lounge, I wanted a drink before I headed home. I knew my wife would be upset I was out so late. It was 4am so the room was almost empty. There were only a couple of guys flirting with some girls. I approached the bar and sat down on a stool. I looked around for the bartender Sasha.

I spotted her at the end of the bar talking with a beautiful chocolate skinned woman with long braids down her back. I knew I'd seen her before. She was the new girl Luciano was always talking about. I must say I was impressed Luciano got this girl to get with him. He must be paying her a grip!

She had a nice body, but not much of an ass. However, what she lacked in ass she made up for in bust. You could tell she was all natural and that was something I liked. Her beauty was unmatched. Inside I knew she didn't belong in a place like this. I also knew I had to have her.

Sasha finally noticed me.

She approached and leaned against the bar.

"Malcolm, long time no see. It's only been, what, a couple of minutes. You must come quick."

I furrowed my brow. "Very funny."

She laughed.

"What can I get you?" she asked placing a napkin down in front of me.

I looked down the bar toward the end, then back at Sasha. "You could give me her name."

She looked around.

"Whose name?" she asked.

I jerked my head in the direction of the braided woman. "Her name."

Sasha followed my motions and looked down the bar. "Who? Kim?"

"Kim," I said smiling. "I like that name."

She shook her head.

"No. I am not hooking you up with Kim. You leave Kim alone."

I raised an eyebrow.

"And why should I do that?" I asked.

"Because she's new and inexperienced..."

"Well, then I get to teach her some new things," I replied.

She was starting to get annoyed.

"Malcolm, what about Ashley?"

I huffed. "What about Ashley? Ashley doesn't own me."

Her eyes went wild. "Maybe not, but she damn well can make Kim's life a living hell."

I thought about that for a second. I looked back down the bar at Kim. She looked up at me. She smiled and my heart skipped a beat.

I looked back over at Sasha. "I'll handle Ashley,"

And I can't wait to take care of Kim.

CHAPTER 6

"Abigail, no clients today?" I asked leaning against the door frame.

She was sitting in one of the VIP rooms watching videos on her smart phone. I gazed at her as she ignored me. I always loved her mocha complexion and long curly hair. She was natural. Nothing on her was fake. You couldn't say that about most of the women in this lounge. It was one of the things I found so attractive about her.

"Abigail...," I said.

She looked up at me for a second and then her eyes traveled back to her phone.

"No," was her quick reply to my question.

I raised an eyebrow. I knew she had at least five clients today. Each one she told she had an STD. Tony found out and exploded. I liked Abigail so I acted quickly, insisting I would talk to her.

"You told your clients you had Syphilis."

"So?" she asked continuing to stare blindly at her cell.

"Tony has hit the roof about it. He's threatening to take any money you earn for the next month leaving you with nothing."

She set her phone down on the table and folded her arms across her chest.

"Fuck Tony," she declared. "He doesn't give a fuck about me or anyone else in this club. "

I could see tears well up in her eyes. She turned her head just as they began to fall. She flicked a tear from her cheek.

I knew she was in a lot of pain. How do you get over finding your best friend dead? Abigail was the one to find Sarah in the back office. She was hysterical after her discovery. On top of that she spent hours being interrogated by police. She didn't show up at work once the club reopened and only returned because of threats from Tony. He needed Abigail here. Besides Ashley and Wendy, Abigail was one of the top earners in the club. She was an asset he was not ready to lose.

I was sent to find her and get her back on track. Tony believed there was no one else that could talk some sense into her. I guess he was relying on me to be persuasive. I must admit, it was one of my strong suits when it came to the girls.

I closed the door after I checked the hallway. I made sure I placed a "Do Not Disturb" sign on the door right before I locked it. I then joined Abigail on the couch. She continued to cry silently and I just let her exorcise the deep ache plaguing her. Finally I pulled her into my arms. She broke down even further into noisy sobs. I held her as her body shook expelling her pain. It took a few minutes before she began to calm down. She pulled back from me and looked me in the eyes.

"Thank you," she said.

I saw she was vulnerable and my sympathy made her see me in a different light. I could tell. She wanted me and I knew that I wanted her too. I let my eyes travel to her plump lips. I needed to taste them. I leaned down to place my lips on hers. Before I could accomplish my goal, she leaned back and pushed me in my chest away from her.

She jumped off the couch pulling down her short red dress and looked…appalled.

"No," she said. "Not gonna happen."

I swallowed the anger and humiliation of her rejection. I closed my eyes and took a few deep breaths. I opened them and smiled raising my hands in surrender.

"Okay, I get it. Nothing is going to happen."

I stood and approached her.

"I just want to give you the comfort that you deserve. When was the last time a man has made love to you? A man that didn't want anything from you?"

She shrugged her shoulders.

"My dear, that's a shame," I took a few steps closer. "I know that is what you need. Especially now. I know that is why you are turning clients away. It must have been so hard to see Sarah that way."

"You have no idea," she said wrapping her arms around herself.

"I know," I continued. "How could anyone understand how that feels?"

I walked past her and headed to the wet bar in the room. Most VIP rooms had one to make the higher end clients more comfortable. I grabbed the vodka and began pouring it into two glasses.

"Why don't you sit down and relax."

She sighed.

"What about Tony. He has me here like I'm a hostage. There is no way I'm going to see clients. You understand. Why can't you tell him how I feel? Tell him I'm afraid that what happened to Sarah will happen to me?"

I smiled to myself as I poured a bunch of crushed up sleeping pills and Xanax into her glass right before pouring in grenadine and pineapple juice.

"Look, don't worry about Tony. I'll handle him. Just loosen up."

I grabbed the drink and turned to her. She was standing with one hand on her hip. When she saw the drink she approached and grabbed it out my hand. Some of it spilled on the carpet.

Damn! I hope there is still enough in the glass.

Without coaxing from me, she devoured the drink. Every last drop cascaded down her beautiful throat. When she was done, I noticed her staring at the glass.

"What is this powder at the bottom?" she asked.

I grabbed the glass and sat it down on the bar.

"Not sure. Must not have been cleaned properly."

"Whatever," she said walking back over to the couch and plopping down. I followed her with my glass of vodka and sat down on the couch next to her. I observed, I watched and I waited for the drugs and the alcohol to kick in. I hoped the "Do Not Disturb" sign on the door would hold off anyone wanting to enter.

I listened for a few minutes as she talked about Tony and finding Sarah dead.

"Who does Tony think he is?" she ranted. "He can't threaten me. I can quit if I want to…"

I could tell she was beginning to slur her words.

"Abi, you're right. You should be able to do what you want to do." I responded placing my hand on her knee.

She smacked my hand off her leg.

I was livid she rebuffed me. I began breathing heavily. I placed my hand back on her leg and began to slide it upward under her dress.

"I told you NO!" she exclaimed standing then falling back down on the couch.

"You don't really mean no," I said moving in closer and placing soft kisses on her cheek. "You want me to touch you."

"No," she argued trying to fend me off as I began to place kisses on her neck. My hands moved back to her leg and I slid it up under her dress.

I knew the pills were taking effect as her eyelids drooped and her head bobbed up and down. She struggled to hold on to her senses. I could have given her more but I hoped for a fight. Yet the amount that was wasted could cause a problem.

She tried again to stand but only managed to slide to the floor. Her dress slid up to her upper thighs making her black thong visible. She lay flat on the floor moaning and groaning. My mouth watered at the thought of lapping up her juices. I bent down in front of her spreading her legs. She tried to knee me in the face but I was able to dodge the attack. I used my fingers to move the material of her underwear to the side. I dodged another knee right before I dropped my head down. My tongue made contact with her clit and I was in heaven. I lapped at her while she moaned the words "No."

In my mind, she was moaning with pleasure so I continued my exploration. Her moans turned into sobs that grew louder in volume. She worked harder to fight the drugs. It only turned me on to feel her body shake and thrust as she attempted to get away from me.

The same feelings I had when I encountered Sarah came back to me. The exhilaration and adrenaline pumping through my veins fueled my desire for more. I sat up wiping my mouth with the back of my hand and gazed at her. She was beautiful. Her long dark curly hair was disheveled and her eyes were glazed over and full of fear. Her terror turned me on further.

Sensuously I caressed her legs letting my fingers stroke her up and down. Suddenly, I felt a jolt of pain erupt on the left side of my face. I fell to the side unclear what just happened. By the time I realized she had kicked me in the face, she was slowly crawling toward the door.

"Help," she tried to scream but it was too faint for anyone to hear.

I moved quickly. I grabbed her ankle and pulled her back toward me across the carpeted floor. She kicked and fought but the more she fought the weaker she became as the drugs began to completely take over.

The battle in her was electrifying and I could feel myself harden. My breathing became labored. I wanted to feel it. I wanted to feel that intense pleasure once again.

"That's right...fight," I said. "Show me what you've got."

I felt invigorated as I straddled her beautiful body. I could still taste her on my lips. It was a shame what had to happen. It was the only way I could feel the ultimate bliss.

I reached on the couch and grabbed a pillow. I placed it over her face and held it there. The sleeping pills were close to knocking her out but that didn't stop her from clawing and scratching at my arms. I felt her nails digging under my skin.

It took longer than I anticipated. It felt like forever but I held the pillow in place. I held it there even when I saw she had went limp and there was no longer any movement from her. I removed the pillow slowly. Placing two fingers on her throat, I felt for a pulse.

There wasn't one.

She was gone.

I was never more ALIVE!

CHAPTER 7

Kenneth

The *Inferno Lounge* was busy and boisterous when I arrived. There were men everywhere and for every guy there were at least two women. I knew Tony had made some new hires. Quite a few girls quit after Sarah was found dead. I noticed there were at least 10 new pretty faces. Yet, none of them appealed to me.

I had an appointment with Wendy this evening and I was pretty excited about that. It had been a long day and an even longer month. I needed a full release. This was my first day back after the lounge reopened. I would have been back sooner but I usually wait until my brother wasn't around and with all that's been going on he has been a permanent fixture here for the past few weeks.

This week he's on vacation with his family, so I called and made arrangements with Wendy. I was finally free to have some fun.

I walked through the lounge and made it to the bar. I sat on a stool and waited for Sasha. I really liked Sasha. She was cool, a rebel, funny and beautiful. She would be a catch for any man and I tried once to make her mine. That is when I found out she only liked women.

Sasha finally approached and sat down a napkin in front of me.

"What can I get you cutie?" she asked one hand on her hip.

I smiled.

"A kiss would be nice," I replied.

She laughed then leaned in real close.

"Unless you got a pussy in those pants, it ain't gonna happen."

I raised an eyebrow.

"So vulgar!" I responded.

"Always," she said with a wink.

"Okay, give me a bourbon and cola."

"You got it," she said.

I watched as she quickly made my drink. She set it down on a napkin in front of me. I took a sip.

"Girl, can I have some cola with this bourbon?"

She laughed.

"Pussy!" she responded.

"Then that means you can give me a kiss," I joked.

She stuck her tongue out at me then laughed. She leaned in again.

"Here to see Wendy?" she asked.

"Yes," I said. "Who else would I see?" I asked taking a sip of my drink.

She cocked her head to the side.

"Anyone else!" she exclaimed. "You deserve much better than Wendy. You deserve much better than this place."

I smiled.

"Aww, Sasha, I didn't know you cared."

"Look," she began. "Wendy is a dirty old skank. You don't need to be here hooking up with somebody's leftovers."

I took a big gulp of my drink then immediately regretted it. The liquid felt like it was burning a hole in my chest. I coughed.

"Sasha, you're sounding like my brother."

"I never thought I would say this but…" She took a deep breath. "Malcolm is right. You should be married to a good woman with three kids surrounded by a white picket fence."

I sighed.

"I'll tell you exactly what I told Malcolm. I'm a grown man and I can take care of myself."

She shook her head.

"Don't say I didn't warn you." She walked away to serve another customer.

I checked my watch. I had 15 minutes before I had to meet with Wendy. I thought about what Sasha said. Neither she nor Malcolm knew I wanted more for myself as well. I just hadn't found the right woman. I knew the odds. Finding her in this place is rare but until I found the woman of my dreams somewhere else, this was the place to have some fun and forget about my troubles.

I scanned the room and noticed there were also some guys here I hadn't seen before. Maybe this was the reason for the new hires so quick. I looked up to see Luciano coming down the stairs holding hands with the most beautiful woman I'd ever laid eyes on.

I knew her. I couldn't forget her. She had long box braids down her back and glowing skin with a heart-stopping smile. Yes, I remember that smile.

Kimberly Lawson.

She was the woman I rescued from that lousy detective. I hadn't seen her since then and after seeing her now, I regretted making arrangements with Wendy. I watched her walk down the stairs and approach the bar.

Luciano followed her. He noticed me and came over. Fortunate for me, she came along.

"Kenneth, how's it going?"

I turned on my stool toward him then stood.

"Luciano, it's going well, man."

I looked at the woman accompanying him.

"I know this beautiful young lady. Kimberly, right?"

She smiled that amazing smile of hers.

"Just call me Kim. Only my parents call me Kimberly," she said. "I remember you. I should. You're apparently my attorney."

Just then we heard glass shatter. In the corner we saw some girls fighting. They were loud and boisterous, knocking over chairs and pulling each other's hair.

Luciano sighed.

"I guess I have to handle that," he said heading toward the fray. He was followed by two of the bouncers.

Once I was alone with Kim, I decided I would get to know her better.

"What brings you here?" I asked and immediately felt really stupid.

Of course you know why she is here, idiot!

She laughed and I was captivated by the sound. It was feminine and quirky.

"Should I ask you that same crazy question?" she asked still laughing.

I laughed as well.

"What I meant to say is how did you end up working here?"

She pursed her lips. Her eyes traveled upward. Then she looked me in the eye.

"I value my future."

I was confused at what she meant.

I folded my arms across my chest. "What do you mean? This is hardly the place where you better yourself."

She folded her arms across her chest.

"Well," she began. "The money I make here helps put me through college. It also puts a roof over my head and food in my belly. Once I'm done with college, I'll leave here and find a better job with some money saved," she said. Then she inhaled and let it out. "That is why I'm
here."

I was impressed. She wasn't like Wendy and Ashley who have made this their careers. She was different. Not that it mattered. I was already smitten.

"So you couldn't find a job that let you have all that and not do this?" I asked.

She squinted her eyes at me and placed her hand on her hip. I could tell my question annoyed her.

"Apparently not," she said.

I smiled at her.

She smiled back.

"Those are good reasons," I said.

For a few seconds we just stared at each other.

Man, she was beautiful!

Suddenly I felt a hand on my shoulder.

"Aren't you going to buy me a drink before you rock my world?" I heard Wendy say into my ear.

I turned and faced her.

"Of course," I said slightly annoyed at the interruption.

For some reason I felt ashamed to have an evening planned with an escort. I couldn't say why since I have never had that feeling before.

"It was nice talking with you," I said turning my attention back to Kim. To my surprise she'd already walked away. There was a sense of longing for her return. I saw her at the end of the bar with Sasha and April, a girl that worked here.

"C'mon Kenneth. Leave the rift-raft and let's go upstairs. I have some new toys I want to show you," Wendy said.

I obediently followed. When we got there we found Luciano, a bouncer and a group of girls shaking and crying. There was pandemonium coming from the room at the end of the hall. I went to follow the commotion but was stopped by Luciano.

"Kenneth, you don't want to go down there."

"What the fuck is going on?" Wendy demanded to know.

"Star," he said pointing to a girl sitting on the floor being comforted by a couple of women. "Found Abigail.

I was confused by what that meant.

"Found Abigail? Doing what?" Wendy questioned.

I looked down the hall and saw the expressions on the men's faces. I looked over at the women and I knew. I grabbed Wendy by the arm and pulled her back against me. Luciano looked at us with his eyes filling up with tears.

"Abigail's dead."

CHAPTER 8

Malcolm

"So you're telling me it was a suicide?" Tony asks taking a sip of vodka.

It was 11 am and he was already drinking. That was usually a sign he was under heavy stress. I understood. We had two deaths at the lounge about a month apart.

Abigail.

Abigail was funny, pretty and smart. She had her entire life ahead of her. Finding out she was dead was a heartbreaker. I guess seeing her best friend deceased was too much for her. I didn't agree with Tony when he made her return to work so soon. He should have known she would be a liability.

"I'm telling you what the police are telling me," I replied.

After Abigail was found, *Inferno* once again became a crime scene and we had to close up shop. However, there were a few cops on our payroll in robbery, narcotics and homicide that kept me in the loop.

In this environment no matter how hard Tony and Luciano try to keep out drugs, they always find a way to make it inside. We've had a few girls overdose in the past. That was when Tony and his dad began paying cops to make these types of things go away. It was well worth the money in my opinion and made my job a little bit easier.

It appeared Abigail had committed suicide. According to the police, the drugs that killed her were things you could find in any household. She was found alone, unconscious with a bottle of over-the-counter sleeping pills and Xanax registered to her right next to her body.

It's a shame. I knew finding Sarah messed her up. Yet, I had no idea she was suicidal. The only person in the room that should have picked up on it was quiet.

"Luc, did you know she was suicidal?" I questioned.

He looked over at me with bloodshot eyes. You could tell he had been crying. I knew that he was attached to the girls but crying was a bit much.

"No, of course not. If I had known she was going to kill herself I would have gotten her help."

He looked over at Tony.

"You made her come back to work. I told you to give her more time."

Tony sighed. He looked over at me.

"So when can the girls come back?" he said ignoring Luciano. "I can't have them around with the police in and out of the building."

"Just give them another day. I was told one more day and they will be out of our hair.

The police are devoting more time to this suicide than to any other they investigate. One reason was they were hoping the longer they stuck around the better their chance were at finding something illegal. Another reason was that another woman was just murdered here only a few weeks ago. They wanted to be sure Abigail died by her own hands and they didn't have a serial killer running around.

"One more day is all I'm giving them. This shit is getting out of hand. Any news about Sarah?"

I didn't have the heart to tell him the police had no leads. I also didn't want to tell him part of the reason they had nothing was mainly our fault. We ordered anyone that worked for the lounge to not talk to the police. If they were ever questioned I ordered them to shut up and ask for me or one of my associates at Bradley, Johnson and Lyle.

"There's nothing so far, Tony."

His nostrils flared.

"WHAT THE FUCK ARE THE POLICE DOING!" he exclaimed slamming his fist on his desk.

"Tony, we run background checks on everyone who comes in here and everyone who works here. No one comes in here without you or I knowing," Luciano said.

He looked calmer now talking to Tony in a more relaxed softer voice. I agreed with him. Either someone was let in that we didn't know about or the crime was an inside job.

"Luciano is right," I said.

Luciano looked at me with both eyebrows raised as if he were surprised I agreed with his logic.

"Tony," he said. "I have a solution."

Tony and I both looked at him. I was intrigued. What solution did he come up with?

"I say we put cameras in the VIP rooms and back offices. Only we can have access to the footage."

"NO!" Tony and I said in unison.

The last thing I needed was video footage of me cheating on my wife. I didn't even let girls I slept with have their cell phones. It was one of the reasons I only slept with Ashley now. The younger girls were attached to their phones and could secretly record.

"Are you out of your fucking mind Luc? We promise our clients secrecy and anonymity. How many clients would we have if it gets out that we tape them doing illegal things like…sleeping with hookers?" Tony said.

Luciano looked like a child being scolded. I didn't know what he was thinking but I had enough for tonight. It had been a long day and I was ready to go.

"Look," I said standing. "I have to head home."

"Keep me posted," Tony said. "Oh, and send Ashley my regards," he said with a smirk.

I shook my head.

I opened the door and walked out. I had no intentions of seeing Ashley tonight. I just needed a good night of sound sleeping. I was feeling low about the death of the two young women. It was a shame that girls so young and full of so much potential lost their lives. I was going to head home and kiss my daughter. I knew I didn't want her ending up in a place like this.

As I walked through the empty lounge, someone on a couch in the corner caught my eye. I stopped and noticed the long braids and the beautiful dark brown skin.

I smiled.

I didn't expect to see anyone here let alone the object of my attraction as of late. I approached and she barely noticed as her eyes stayed locked on her cell phone. I took a seat next to her and she still barely even registered I was there.

"So, what are you doing here? The lounge is closed."

Startled, she looked up at me with eyes wide.

"Oh, Umm…" she stammered. "When did you get here?"

These young girls and their phones.

"I sat down while you were on social media."

She rolled her eyes.

"I wasn't on social media. I was reading a text from my mother."

"Well, how is dear old mom?" I asked leaning back against the cushions.

She squinted her eyes at me.

"My mom is fine. Is there something I can help you with?" she asked.

I knew exactly what she could help me with. I noticed she had a little bit of attitude in her voice. I liked that.

"I was just wondering why you were here? Most of the girls are at home or working out of the hotel," I asked leaning in closer.

"Well, Luciano is my client tonight and I'm waiting for him."

I furrowed my brow.

"I don't understand why he's your only client. You need to branch out baby."

"I'll branch out when someone requests me."

"That's all you need is a request?" I asked.

"Isn't that how it works?"

I smiled. She was quick with the replies. She was smart and quick witted. Something I could work with.

Suddenly Luciano walked over with a frown on his face. Either he was not happy I was talking to Kim or he was still reeling from being chewed out by Tony.

"Kim, are you ready?" he asked.

No matter how upset he appeared, he spoke to her in a gentle soothing tone.

She grabbed her phone, stood and fixed her short skirt. Her beautiful chocolate legs caught my attention. I wondered what they would look like wrapped around my waist.

"It was nice talking to you, Kim." I said.

She frowned.

"How did you know my name?" she asked.

I smiled.

"Luciano just said it."

"Oh…yeah," she said with a laugh.

It was the most amazing laugh I had ever heard.

"It was nice talking to you too...um…I didn't catch your name."

I stood and reached out my hand. She placed her hand in mine. I pulled it to my lips and placed a soft kiss on the back.

"It's Malcolm, sweetie."

She raised an eyebrow.

"Malcolm, don't call me sweetie," she said with a smile.

Then she walked away with Luciano trailing behind.

CHAPTER 9

Kimberly

"It's no use," Luciano said defeated.

I looked up at him and sighed.

We had been at this for 45 minutes. I stripped for him, which is something I don't normally do, and I masturbated for him. Now, I kneeled in front of him holding his flaccid penis in my hand trying to breathe life into it. Nothing I did would get him erect.

"Maybe if I try something else…"

I felt bad he was impotent. I knew it frustrated him he couldn't have sex with women the way he wanted to and I tried to help but I was starting to agree with him. There seemed to be no use.

"We can just try again later," he replied standing and putting on his pants.

I sat on my heels half naked and watched him pace around the room for a minute. His eyebrows were furrowed and his lips trembled.

I checked the digital clock on the side table in his office and realized I had an appointment with a new client in two hours. I was told this morning by the owner Tony, who never said two words to me, that someone wanted me as a "companion." That shocked me. Immediately after finding out I went into the bathroom and vomited up my fears.

I had solely been with Luciano for almost two months. I knew the more I was out there the more likely I would be requested. I kept my head down and only surfaced when it was almost time for my shift to end. I also had a feeling Luciano was turning guys down when they asked to see me. I was grateful for that. However, I knew it would be a matter of time before he would no longer be able to do that. I dreaded that day.

I stood and began to dress. I threw on my tank top and some jeans.

"I have to go Luciano," I said sliding my feet into a pair of flip flops.

He came over to me and slipped his arms around my waist.

"You don't have to go out there. You can hide out in here."

I wish that I could, but I had a real client today that I'm sure wanted to do more than just go down on me. At the thought, I threw up a little in my mouth.

"I can't do that. Apparently, there is a VIP request for me today."

He let me go and took a step back.

"A VIP?" he asked. "I didn't get any request."

"Tony said they requested me through him."

He looked shocked, devastated and heartbroken.

I knew why he was so dismayed. April explained to me how requests work. The lounge only works through request by men approved by Luciano and then by Tony. They are given background checks and health screenings. They also pay a hefty yearly fee. According to her, a client can make a request two ways. They can either request to see a girl through Luciano or Tony. A normal request is made through Luciano. It is rare that a girl is requested through Tony and asked to be the only companion of any man. If a man decides he only wants that girl, then he forfeits the privilege of seeing any other women. It's almost like turning that woman into a mistress you only see at the club.

A request through Tony, however, does not automatically make this happen. The VIP requests the girl. They have an encounter and then the guy decides if he wants her to be his "sole companion."

That is why Luciano was so upset. If this client liked me, there was a chance he wouldn't be able to sleep with me anymore. I had no clue whether this was a good thing or a bad thing. I knew that I trusted Luciano and I didn't know who this new stranger was.

I was stunned someone requested me through Tony. I didn't think I was here long enough or out in the public enough to have someone jump through hoops and ask for me.

I exited Luciano's office while he just sat in his chair staring at the wall. I felt really bad for him. According to Sasha he doesn't really mess with the women in the club and none of them really deal with him. I felt awful for him but I felt worse for myself. I went up to the second floor bathroom to shower and get ready for my new client. I was nervous and unstable. I had to redo my lipstick twice. The thought of this client scared me shitless. I tried to pump myself up before I went downstairs still shaking.

This is the moment you see if you can really do this job. This is the fucking moment!

I entered the curtained off area in the lounge where Tony always sat entertaining guests. This evening he was there drinking and chatting with this gorgeous dark skin black man. I had the same reaction I had the first day I saw him. I felt light headed. His appearance took my breath away. He was very tall with a lean body and a great smile. His eyes and his dimples were familiar.

When they noticed me they both stood.

"Finally," Tony said. "Here's your girl."

He approached me and I shuddered. He reached out and put his hands on my shoulders.

"Whoa," he said looking into my eyes. "Are you cold?"

I shook my head.

He smiled. He leaned down and placed a kiss on my cheek.

The way he was treating me was weird. In a normal world, this would be chivalrous and something I would adore in a man. But in this place, men treated women like property not like actual women.

"It's really good to see you again, Kim," he said.

"I'm really glad to see you too, Kenneth" I replied.

He smiled at that. I think he was glad I remembered him. But who could forget that sexy smile and those gorgeous brown eyes.

I was seriously happy to see him. I had no clue who my client would or could be and I was glad it was someone I had met before. Plus it didn't hurt that he was so hot!

"Ken, here's your room key," Tony said handing him a card. "Kim will meet you up there in a few minutes."

Kenneth grabbed the key, smiled and left the room. Once he was gone, Tony moved in on me.

"Look, he is a very special client. I normally keep new girls away from my preferred customers, but he requested you."

He reached out and grabbed my arm pulling me close to him.

"You're hurting me." I said trying to pull myself from his grasp.

"This is nothing compared to what I'll do to you if you fuck this up. Now, he is in room 203. Get up there."

He let me go but I just stood there pissed off. I refused to have someone talk to me like that.

"What the fuck are you waiting for?" he asked folding his arms across his chest.

I stood firm and placed my hands on my hips.

"I'm waiting for you to apologize."

When the words left my mouth, I instantly wanted to take them back. He was still in charge and he had the power to make sure I got all the disgusting nasty guys. Yet, I knew I still had the power to quit. Leaving this place wouldn't be the worst thing in the world.

He looked livid. I am pretty sure no other woman has spoken to him like this before. I took a step back worried he may assume he is a pimp and try to act as such. Then he surprised me even more. He started to laugh.

"You're right," he said. "I apologize."

I wasn't expecting an apology.

"You do?"

"Yes, I do," he said closing the gap between us.

He moved in so close I thought he was going to kiss me. And he did placing his lips on mine softly then hungrily. He put his hand on the back of my head and we kissed for a few seconds. Then he leaned back.

"Hmmm, sweet. Luciano has been keeping a prize to himself all this time," he remarked.

I was shaken. He had barely said anything to me since I started working here and I was told by April that was a good thing. I should stay off his radar. What would April think about what just transpired here?

He leaned in like he wanted to kiss me again but instead he brought his lips to my ear.

"You're so fucking sexy and I want to keep you around for awhile," Then he grabbed me by the forearm and pulled my body against his. "But, if you ever talk to me like that again…you'll fucking regret it."

He left the room and I stood there completely freaked. That feeling did not leave as I stood in front of the door leading to the room that held my new client.

This is my one real client and I didn't know what he liked. I wasn't sure how to even find out what he liked. April said I thought about it too much. She insisted I just see him as a normal man and bang him like crazy.

"Don't think, just fuck," she told me.

I dressed in a black lacy bra and panties. I wore a silk robe covering myself until Kenneth had the chance to undress me. My dark chocolate legs were freshly shaved and I knew I would be any man's dream tonight. I thought I would keep it simple. If he is into fantasy then there was a trunk full of things we could play with.

When I got to the room the door was closed. I stood outside in the hall trying to get up the courage to walk inside. I think I stood there for at least ten minutes before someone tapped me on the shoulder. It was April.

"What the hell are you doing?" she asked.

I could tell she was on the way to visit a client as well. She was wearing a red teddy with red fish net stockings and a red wig. She had on these long red press-on-nails and wore school girl pig tails. When I saw her…I started laughing.

"What am I doing?" I replied. "What the hell are you doing? Are you really walking around like this?"

She slapped my arm.

"Ow!" I exclaimed.

"I am on my way to meet a client. You need to get in there and get with yours."

"I'm nervous." I whispered.

Shaking her head, she reached over quickly and opened the door. Then with all her might she started to push me in the room.

"April, no" I whispered.

She pushed me inside and closed the door.

It was dark but I could see him sitting on the bed. He was still fully clothed so that was a plus for me. I stood there trying to figure out what to do with my body.

"Come sit over here with me," he said.

I was grateful he initiated contact. I walked over and sat down on the bed next to him.

He moved closer. I could feel my knees begin to shake. He placed his hand on my thigh.

"So what do you want me to do?" I asked staring at his hand on my knee.

"First," he began. He eyes went up and down my body. "I want to know, how are you?"

That threw me off.

"Umm…I…I'm okay," I stammered.

"Don't be nervous. I was hoping we could take it slow."

Hearing those words made me feel better. I started to relax just a little. I took a deep breath and smiled. I was grateful this man wanted to take his time with me.

"Of course." I answered.

He reached up and slowly began to caress my face with the back of his hand. His hand glided down my neck and then down my body. He reached the knot that kept my robe closed and undid it. I felt the cold air hit my body. I shuddered.

He cocked his head to the side and smiled.

"I promise I won't hurt you," he claimed.

I let out the breath I didn't know I was holding.

He leaned in closer and kissed me gently on my neck again and again. I felt his tongue glide across my collarbone. He continued to go lower until he reached my breasts. He cupped one in his hand. His mouth followed and he licked my nipple through the lacy fabric. A moan escaped my lips.

He looked up at me and smiled. I could feel my panties getting soaked. He sat up and brought his lips to mine. His kiss was soft and gentle and made me feel safe and secure. I scooted closer and wrapped my arms around his neck. His hand came to my back and he caressed me gently. We kissed for a few minutes until finally he pulled back.

"Wow," he said.

I giggled.

"Did you feel that?" He asked rubbing his hand on my legs.

I knew exactly what he was talking about. There was a spark that shook my body the moment we kissed. I'm not sure if that was supposed to happen between a man and his prostitute.

We decided to try it again to see if we got the same response. We kissed and I didn't want to stop. I loved the way he smelled, the way he tasted and I didn't want to let him go.

We ended up lying across the bed touching and caressing each other. He eventually removed his shirt and I could see his beautiful chocolate body better. I could tell he was a man that worked out and it all paid off. I rubbed my hands across his muscular chest as we kissed.

His mouth laid kisses down my body and I moaned imagining I was not a companion in a lounge. I was just a woman and he was just a man and we were enjoying sex as any couple would.

I was already half naked so it didn't take much for him to relieve me of the rest of my clothing. When done, he undressed himself. He returned to me and slid his body between my legs. I wrapped them around his waist and then we kissed again. He gently caressed my body as he placed kisses down my neck. I unraveled my legs from around his waist as he licked the valley between my breasts. I moaned as his hand slid between the meeting of my thighs and stroked me there. His lips found mine again and our tongues found each other. He tasted sweet and I was intoxicated with how he made me feel.

He slipped two fingers inside of me and I moaned with pleasure.

He continued to kiss down my body stopping to take a firm nipple into his mouth. He wrapped his tongue around one and then the other. I was so turned on and wanted him inside of me. Yet, he took his time exploring and teasing. Finally he dropped his head between my legs and began to taste me.

"Oh, that feels so good." I moaned.

"Well, you taste so good, so we're even," he sat up and replied.

He went back to pleasing me and I placed my hands on his head as his tongue caressed my clit. He placed two fingers inside of me as he licked and sucked. I was coming and I didn't want to come so quick. There was no use in fighting it, however. I came hard squeezing my legs shut and locking him in position. I finally released and he sat up.

"I thought I was never coming out of that death grip."

I laughed.

"I haven't come that hard in a long time."

He laughed.

"I find that hard to believe," he said smiling.

He reached down and grabbed a condom from his pants pocket and put it on.

Then he was on top of me. He entered me slowly then picked up the pace. I kept up with him closing my eyes to feel the pleasure more intensely. Deeper he went lifting my leg onto his shoulder.

Suddenly his pace increased and I held on by gripping the sheets.

I came again. It snuck up on me and I was left breathless. I screamed out and he pounded harder. He groaned and came inside of me.

When his orgasm was over he collapsed on the bed. We laid there listening to each other breathe.

Finally, he spoke.

"So…that was amazing."

I laughed.

"It was,' I agreed.

He reached over and pulled me into his arms. He held me there and I relaxed letting myself melt into him.

"When I saw you and talked with you…I knew you were special," he said running his fingers up and down my back.

"I wanted to get to know you. I wanted to touch you. I wanted to…"

"You wanted to fuck me." I said.

He dropped his head and sighed.

"Yes," he replied. I also want more than that. I would like to get to know you."

I could hear April in my head telling me that was a bad idea. She warned me about getting too attached to a client. I'm never to see them outside of the club.

"Isn't that against attorney-client something or other?"

He laughed.

"No, but if it were, we have gone well beyond that."

Well, it's against the rules at this place.

"Kenneth, I'll think about it," I replied. "Right now I just need my payment."

He seemed a little dejected by my request, yet he moved from the bed and dug around in his pants for his wallet. He came back handing me a wad of bills.

"Now that we got that unpleasantness out of the way, I am going to court you like a gentleman should."

"Court me?" I said laughing.

"Yes," he replied. "I am going to bring you flowers and buy you chocolates…"

I giggled.

"What's so funny?" he asked.

I laid there listening to all of the things a gallant man wanted to do for me thinking…*what did I get myself into?*

CHAPTER 10

Kimberly

Inferno Lounge doesn't only have male clients. A fair number of women frequented the lounge looking for female companionship. Most of them were women married to men looking for something outside their everyday mundane lives. The anonymity of the lounge gave them the opportunity to enjoy themselves without fear of the rest of the world finding out.

I never engaged with the women. Not that I hadn't thought about it. April knew all about my hang-ups. She knew my parents and how they were against homosexuality. Then again they were also against prostitution. When I was in Middle School, I experimented with a friend of mine. I was so ashamed of my actions I never tried it again, though I always thought about that time in my life.

April told me I needed to get over it and grab a female client while I had the chance. According to her, the female clients pay more and tended to treat the girls better than the men. Deep down, I wanted to take advantage of the opportunity. However, my shame turned me into a coward and whenever the women showed up, I hid in Luciano's office or in a dark corner in the back of the main room…like I'm doing now.

Tonight was ladies night and a few of Tony's female VIPs arrived for a special evening. Luciano told me that some of the women requested Tony shut down the lounge and have a night where the women could occupy the building without the male clients trying to sleep with them or have threesomes with them and other girls. Tony obliged and for once I had a night at work where I actually felt safe. Especially since Tony was in the building. When he was here security looked out for us instead of slacking off and sleeping with girls. They were actually securing the place.

My shame wasn't the only reason I was in hiding. The days the women were here…so were Ashley and Wendy. When they worked they always seemed to suck the air out of the room. I never wanted to be here when they were on the clock. They would glare at me whenever they got the chance or found ways to "accidentally" spill drinks on me. It was infuriating but April insisted I hold my tongue and keep my head down.

So I sat in the corner while Wendy and Ashley fawned over a woman at the bar. It was April's night off so we personal messaged over social media.

"Ashley and Wendy look a hot mess," I sent.

"As usual…" she replied. "Is she wearing that worn out red dress with the gold heels?"

I looked up from my phone and leaned over so I could get a better view of the bar. I saw Ashley in the red dress and burst into laughter. I had to place my hand over my mouth before I was noticed.

I was so focused on my phone and the funny messages April sent that I didn't see who was walking over. When they plopped down on either side of me, I jumped and dropped my phone in the process. I looked from side to side at Wendy and Ashley. I swallowed the lump in my throat.

"Damn bitch! Why are you so jumpy?"Ashley asked.

They squeezed even closer to me and I began to feel claustrophobic. I turned to the side to look at Ashley.

"Well, I tend to be jumpy when people sneak up on me," I replied bending down to pick up my phone.

"How has your evening been going so far?" Wendy asked.

I knew these women didn't like me. They made that perfectly clear by ignoring me and when they did acknowledge me it was to put me down or make fun of me. So why are they cozying up to me now? I had good reason to be suspicious.

"My evening has been fine," I answered.

Ashley placed her hand on my knee and smiled.

"I'm just going to get to the point," she began. "We have a female client that would like a foursome with me, Wendy and…you."

My eyes grew wide at her words.

"You won't have to eat pussy or anything just be willing to have your pussy ate."

I dropped my phone again. Wendy leaned down to pick it up but she didn't give it to me. She just held it in her hand. I looked from side to side at the both of them.

"I don't think I heard you correctly," I said. "You want me to have a foursome with you?"

"It's more like we are giving you the opportunity to get in on a high-end client for a change. Just sleeping with Luciano isn't going to get you nowhere," Ashley claimed.

I thought about that. Being with Luciano wasn't pulling in that much money. I pay rent, my tuition and that's it. However, I would rather continue to sleep with Luciano then get in bed with these two. I knew that most girls wouldn't turn them down even if they wanted to. I wasn't most girls. I understood, however rejecting their offer could bring me some trouble. Yet there was no way I was going to go through with this.

"I can't…I can't do it,"

"C'mon, there is a lot of money at stake. As you can see she's very wealthy," Wendy replied.

"I said no."

They looked at each other then back at me.

"I told you we should have pulled in one of the new hires," Wendy said through gritted teeth. "I had to be nice to this bitch for nothing."

Ashley glared at her.

"She doesn't want one of them. She apparently wants…this thing," she said pointing at me.

They talked to each other as if I wasn't sitting between them.

Wendy stood and fixed her dress. Then she looked at me.

"This was your opportunity to make up for trying to steal my client. Now you are back on my radar, skank," she said waving my phone around in the air.

I had no clue what she was talking about. I just kept my eyes on my phone.

"Oh yeah," Ashley said standing and turning to me. She folded her arms across her chest. "You're trying to move up by stealing clients." She shook her head. "That shit ain't going down."

I still had no idea what they were talking about but I knew I didn't like them standing over me. I went to stand and Wendy pushed hard sending me plopping back down on the couch.

"Take this as your only warning, uppity bitch. Stay the fuck away from Kenneth," Wendy said.

"Learn the rules now or we will make your life a living hell in and out of the lounge," Ashley threatened.

I looked up at them feeling anger and humiliation. They loomed over me daring me to get up.

All because of Kenneth?

I went to stand again and Wendy pushed me back down. They both laughed. I was furious.

"Don't touch me!" I ordered.

My nostrils flared and my hands balled into fists.

"What are you going to do?" Wendy asked.

Ashley laughed.

I was too furious to speak.

"C'mon, Wendy. This is fun but we have a client to get to," Ashley said.

Wendy glared at me no longer smiling. She tossed my phone. It hit the couch, bounced off and landed on the ground. The case protecting the phone broke off into pieces on the floor.

"Oops!" Wendy said laughing.

Then she and Ashley walked away from me. I looked over and saw some of the newer girls staring and laughing. As I sat on my knees picking up all the pieces of my phone case, I knew that was the last time I would sit back and let them bully me. I would do whatever I wanted to do and see whomever I wanted to see.

It was time for the Queen bitch and her court jester's reign to be over!

CHAPTER 11

Malcolm

The lounge in the day time was a different looking place. The chairs were set on the tables and the place was not full of sexy women and men with pockets full of cash. Instead there were cleaning ladies and men scrubbing the place spotless. Sasha was always there. I waved at her on my way to Tony's office. She insisted she clean the bar not wanting anyone to mess things up.

Tony was around on days like this as well. He used the time to check the books and look for other ways to make money. One of his dreams was to own multiple lounges. I wasn't too fond of the idea. He could barely keep this place in check. What would he do with more than one?

When I walked into his office, I found him along with Luciano. Tony was sitting behind his desk crouched over his laptop and Luciano was behind him looking over his shoulder staring at whatever Tony was working on.

They both looked startled when I strolled in.

"Malcolm! What brings you here? I wasn't expecting you and there is no ass around. What can I do for you?" Tony questioned.

I came bringing information about Sarah and Abigail. I wasn't sure exactly if it was good or bad news. I spent the morning discussing the case over coffee with two officers I've known a long time and who have been on Tony and his dad's payroll longer than that.

"Tony, Luc, just the men I want to see." I said sitting down in the chair across from Tony. "I have some news about Sarah and Abigail."

They both gave me their full attention. Luc sat in the seat next to me and Tony closed his laptop.

"The Medical Examiner confirmed that Sarah was strangled and has officially ruled her death a homicide," I said.

Tony pursed his lips together. I knew he was imagining what poor Sarah had been through.

"Apparently they ran a toxicology report on Sarah and Abigail. Both women were found to have large amounts of sleeping pills and Xanax in their system," I continued.

Tony looked confused. "What does that mean?" he asked.

"How can that be? I know Abigail killed herself with those drugs but how did Sarah have them in her system as well?" Luciano asked.

I took a deep breath and let it out.

"Well, the police believe, and this is just a hunch on their part, Sarah and Abigail's deaths are connected and not in the way we think." I replied.

I took another deep inhale and exhale before I finished.

"The Xanax we know belonged to Abigail. There was a bottle of it with her name on it right next to her when she was found. Abigail may not have killed herself because she found Sarah. She found Sarah because SHE was the one that killed her."

The room was silent for a few seconds as the information I relayed sunk in. Luciano dropped his head and Tony still looked as though he didn't understand a word I said. It was a lot to take in. Though the police were not closing the case and were still investigating, this was the consensus around the precinct.

"They believe Abigail killed Sarah?" Luciano asked.

I nodded.

"But how could she possibly do that?" he asked.

"Well," I began. "If Sarah was drugged, then it would have been easy for her to strangle her."

"That was not what I meant," said Luciano. "I want to know how she could do that? They were really close. I cannot see Abi hurting Sarah."

I agreed with him. I thought the police needed to go back to the drawing board on this one. Yet it seemed like it was the only thing that made sense at the moment. Tony was leaning back in his seat quiet. I knew he was having a hard time with this information. Sarah and Abi were close to him. Then a thought hit me. What if Abi and Tony were too close? What if Abigail wanted Sarah out of the way?

"Look, I just figured I would come and tell you this in person. They are not done investigating but I promised you that whenever I heard something I would keep you posted."

"Yeah, Malcolm," he said waving his hand at me.

I stood and nodded at Luciano before I left Tony's office. The mood was now sour and there was only one thing that would cheer me up…

I heard laughter coming from the back of the lounge as I exited the office. I turned to see Sasha, April one of the older women that worked at the club. To my delight, sitting with them was the beautiful Kim. I knew I would have to say hello before I left.

I moved toward them. April noticed me first and signaled to the other women I was approaching. They looked up at me.

"Well, hello beautiful ladies."

Sasha rolled her eyes.

"Hey Malcolm," April said.

I waited for Kim to reply. She didn't say a word. I raised an eyebrow.

"Someone's being rude."

She finally looked up with a smile.

"I was waiting for you to greet me by my name, sweetie," she said.

I laughed. "I apologize beau-I mean Kim."

"Thank you," she said.

"What's up Malcolm?" April interrupted. "What can we do for you?"

"I just wanted to say hi, do I have to have ulterior motives?"

Sasha laughed. "You've always got something up your sleeve. Malcolm Johnson doesn't just say 'HI'."

"Okay, you've got me. I was hoping I could speak to Kim…alone."

Sasha and April looked at each other. They then looked at Kim who looked like a deer in headlights.

"Umm No," April said standing. "Kim and I are about to leave. Aren't we?"

Kim didn't answer. She opened her mouth to speak and then shut it. She then stood. They both walked past me and headed for the front entrance double doors.

"Kim! Kim!" I yelled as I followed them.

April kept walking but Kim stopped and walked over to me. I looked over and saw April's hands on her waist.

"Malcolm, what can I do for you?" Kim asked in the sweetest voice.

"I want to know…are you prepared to leave the life you've been living and make a new one with me?"

Her eyes again were wide.

"I have no clue what you're talking about," she replied.

I leaned in close.

"I want to give you what you've been missing with Luciano."

She rolled her eyes and shook her head.

"I'm not missing anything when I am with Luciano," she insisted.

"Oh really?" I asked.

I grabbed her and pulled her close to me. Her body was against mine. I thought at first she was going to move. She didn't. She stayed there in my arms.

"I want to fuck you senseless. I want to push you against the wall while you wrap your legs around me. I want to fuck you hard and rough making you come harder than you've ever come before."

She licked her lips but didn't say a word.

I felt the electricity that flowed between us. It was powerful and I knew I needed more of it. I leaned down and kissed her softly on the lips. She didn't move. We kissed and my tongue hungrily sought hers.

Suddenly I felt a jerk and she was ripped from me. When I opened my eyes April was pulling Kim toward the door and Sasha was standing there.

"Malcolm, I told you no," Sasha said.

"Sasha, I'm a grown ass man. I can do what I want, who I want, when I want."

She opened her mouth to speak.

"I fucking told you I can take care of Ashley."

She walked away from me toward the bar. She was pissed but I didn't care.

I didn't care what anyone said. I was going to make Kim mine.

I smiled.
I could still taste her on my lips.

CHAPTER 12

Kimberly

As with any bad decisions, regret follows close behind. I felt those emotions about my new profession. Tony called and told me I needed to be at the club today on my day off. I had a new client request. Another VIP wanted to see me.

I sat in the middle of my bed and regretted my choice. I deserved a better life for myself. I looked over at my desk in the corner of the room. I saw the stack of books and remembered. My education. I had no other way to pay for school or find a job that could pay me as much as this one could. It felt good to go to the registrar's office and pay for my classes without a loan.

I took a deep breath and let it out. I climbed off the bed and got dressed. I drove the 15 minutes from mine and April's house to the club. There were a plethora of cars in the parking lot and I wondered which one belonged to my new client.

I walked into the lounge and headed straight for the bar. I wasn't much of a drinker but the bar and my little corner seemed to be where I was most comfortable in this place. I knew I relaxed at the bar because of Sasha.

She was better than April at making me feel better about my plight. I was looking for her reassuring aura tonight.

She was serving a customer when I arrived. I looked up at the clock. I was due upstairs with my client in an hour. I felt nauseous. Sasha eventually came over to me. She handed me a shot of vodka. I downed it without question. The liquid was a shock to my system and burned as it went down.

"Look," she said leaning against the counter. "You can always quit this job."

I shook my head.

"I'll quit once I graduate from college debt free."

"Kim, I know April makes it seem like working here is no big deal but this place can destroy people. This may not be the place for you. There is no shame in getting a student loan."

I knew there was "no shame" but I saw how much my parents struggled with debt and how limited they were in doing the things they wanted to do in life. My mother had always longed to travel. Yet, she's too bogged down in debt to do that. I didn't want that for myself. I wanted to graduate debt free, get a job and help them. That was my dream. They're why I do this.

"Sasha, thanks for the advice but I need to do it this way."

She shook her head.

"No one ever listens to me," she mumbled walking away to serve another customer.

I laughed.

I climbed off the stool and made my way upstairs. I showered and dressed in the sexiest lingerie I owned. It was a dark green lace and sheer top with a lacy thong. I threw on a silk robe and walked down the hall to room 206.

I took a deep breath and opened the door. I walked inside a dark room. My anxiety went through the roof.

My thoughts went to the two women who had died in this lounge since I started working here. That didn't make me feel any better about entering this dark room with who knows who.

Suddenly a lamp flicked on and I was greeted by a familiar face.

"Come on over here baby," Malcolm said patting the spot on the bed next to him. "I don't bite. Well, sometimes."

I hesitantly walked over. After our encounter at the lounge a few days ago, April warned me about getting involved with him. She said he was Ashley's client and taking money out of her pocket would bring trouble. To be honest, I was so sick of Ashley this and Wendy that. When they humiliated me in front of people in the lounge I vowed I wouldn't allow them to do that to me again. If their clients wanted me that was their problem...not mine.

Plus, I thought Malcolm was so hot. He had me shaking after our kiss. I didn't expect the reaction I had. The only thing that had me hesitant about getting involved with him was his brother. I didn't realize he and Kenneth were brothers until April told me. I was shocked and then dismayed when she said the brothers were off limits.

Yet, she didn't know the magic that happened between Kenneth and me when we touched. There was a spark I couldn't explain. I told no one about his wanting to date me. That confession from him surprised me. I had no clue if he really meant what he said. It was the reason, no matter how hot he was, why I felt uneasy having Malcolm here waiting for me.

Not feeling like I could just walk away, I dropped my robe to the floor, sat down next to him and placed my hands in my lap.

He smiled.

"Oh, don't be so shy with me. I could tell by our kiss you want me as much as I want you."

He moved closer. His hand came to my chin and he leaned in to kiss me. Our mouths met and he tasted like red wine. I could tell by the way he kissed…he was a forceful lover. His hand came to the back of my head. He conquered me. He treated me as if he owned me. Like I already belonged to him.

He pulled back abruptly and pushed me back onto the bed. He stood and began to strip down. I watched him propped up on my elbows. When he was done he came back to me and positioned himself between my legs. He lifted my lace shirt and wasted no time taking one nipple into his mouth. I winced and groaned as he bit down on one firm nipple. I moaned as he moved over to the other and took as much of my large breast as he could into his mouth.

"Oh, that feels so good," I said.

He continued his exploration of my body by moving downward placing kisses wherever he went.

"Scoot up some on the bed," he said.

I followed his request and moved up on the bed until I was in the middle. He slid my panties down my legs. He tossed them over his shoulder. I laid back anticipating his tongue on me. I was surprised when I felt his fingers enter me first. He roughly pushed them in. I moaned as he found my g-spot and stroked me there.

"You like it rough, I see. That's how I like it too."

Finally his tongue made contact with the wet lips of my pussy. He teased, licking me but left my clit with no attention.

"Please," I groaned.

I heard him chuckle.

"Be patient," he ordered.

Suddenly his tongue plunged inside of me. He fucked me with his tongue before finding my clit. I gripped the sheets as he devoured me. He sucked vigorously on my clit. I could feel my orgasm build, ready to erupt. My hands went to his head and he didn't stop me. I came hard against his mouth. I didn't have time to relish in my pleasure, however. I heard him unwrapping a condom and put it on. Then he was on top of me between my legs. He leaned down and kissed me. Then without warning his right hand was around my throat. He slowly squeezed my windpipe. I began to struggle to breathe. I started to panic. My hands came up to his and I began to pull at them.

"Calm down," he said.

He loosened his grip a little. I tried composing myself but my mind went back to the women that died in the lounge and my fear wouldn't go away. I was sure my brown eyes were wide and terrified.

He continued to constrict my breathing as he entered me. He was large and I felt him squeeze his way inside. I heard him moan and finally he released me. My lungs rushed to fill with air.

I should have been afraid of this man. He apparently liked to strangle women while he fucked. Instead, my mind drifted to the pleasure I felt and all rational thought vanished. I wrapped my legs around his waist as he slammed me. He stopped suddenly and pulled out.

"Turn over," he demanded.

I did as I was told. I flipped over and put my ass into the air. He thrust inside and my legs collapsed.

"C'mon, put that ass up."

I reached out and grabbed two pillows and pushed them underneath me. My legs were still jelly from my last orgasm. That didn't stop another orgasm from building. He hit my g-spot and I struggled to hold on as he continued to fuck me. I came hard gripping the sheets on the bed. He continued to pound me gripping my waist in the process. A strong slap on the ass brought me back into the world.

"Don't quit on me now!" he exclaimed.

He slapped me again with such force I cried out in pain.

"Oh you can take it," he responded.

I heard him groan loudly. He began to grip my neck again. His large hand seized me with such force I fought to breathe. I stayed calm knowing there was nothing I could do. He could kill me. I couldn't even scream...

His pace increased until suddenly he came with a growl.

He released me and then collapsed on the bed. The room was silent except for our heavy breathing.

"Fuck, girl," he said. "You're amazing!"

I smiled and rubbed my neck where he squeezed. It ached and I knew it would leave a bruise. He rolled off the bed and picked up his pants. He pulled out his wallet and retrieved money from it. He handed it to me and I hesitated. Up until this point I was only taking money from Luciano and once from Kenneth. This felt different somehow. With them, I didn't really feel like an escort. With Malcolm...

If I took this money. It would be real. I began to shake.

"What's wrong?" he asked.

I couldn't answer him. I couldn't address the level of emotion I was feeling. The sex was amazing. But I knew there was no real emotion behind it. This was beyond casual. This was professional. I took a deep breath and grabbed the money from his hand.

With that, the choice was finally made. And with every decision I've come to lately there was going to be some guilt and regret.

CHAPTER 13

Malcolm

Peppermints.

That's what she smelled like.

Every chance I got I took in a huge inhale of her scent. I'm not sure if it was the lotion she was wearing or what, but that smell has lingered with me all day.

Kim was an amazing woman and turned me on more than I thought I could handle. I couldn't wait until the next time I had her. It's been awhile since I'd been this excited about being with a woman. I was fixated on her dark brown skin. The amazing way her body felt against mine stayed on my mind. My work day was spent thinking about her. I couldn't explain my actions and my emotions. I shocked Tony by putting in a request to have her solely. I didn't want any man, not Luciano or anyone else touching her.

Today, I sat through a deposition, three meetings and barely retained an ounce of what I heard. My head was full of thoughts of being with Kim again. When I was finally able to focus, I decided to grab myself a cup of coffee. The mocha peppermint coffee creamer reminded me of her. My head was back there in that room with my dick buried deep inside.

My hope was to come home after work, have dinner, see my wife off to bed, and head back to *Inferno* to see Kim. I checked and tonight she was on the clock. Right before I could leave work, another meeting was scheduled and I was late getting home. When I arrived at my house, I noticed my brother's car.

Damn! I forgot he was coming over for dinner. That would make getting to Kim a little more difficult.

As soon as I walked through the door, I was bombarded with the hugs and kisses of my children. I was also confronted by an angry wife. I knew she would be upset I was not on time for dinner.

"Malcolm you're late," Evelyn said. "I had to reheat the food waiting for you."

I hung up my jacket and picked up my son. I followed my wife and my daughter into the dining room.

"Next time just get started without me."

I looked around.

"Where's Kenneth?" I asked.

"Right here," he said coming from behind me into the room.

I placed my son into his highchair. I walked over and pulled my wife into an embrace. I kissed her on the lips. Her face was still set into a frown.

"Don't look at me like that," I requested. "I'll call next time."

She huffed.

"There better not be a next time," she said. "You spend all your time working all day and then all night for Tony at his lounge. The least you can do is be home in time for dinner."

I sighed. I wasn't in the mood for this argument now.

"I'll try to be home on time," I replied. *Unless something comes up*, I thought.

She sighed and walked out of the dining room area over to the kitchen. I helped my daughter into her chair. I gave her a raspberry on her cheek. She giggled.

"Baby bro," I said finally greeting Kenneth. "What's up?" I asked sitting down at the front end of the table.

"Nothing much," he said placing his napkin in his lap. " Just the usual. I have an arraignments of a couple clients in the morning, then a few more cases to go over."

"Bro, you work too much. Any dates with any women planned?" I asked.

My brother spends so much time working, he never has time for a social life and when he does have any free time he tries to show up at the lounge. I wanted to put a stop to that.

"No. No dates Malcolm. Why are you always trying to be a part of my love life?"

Evelyn returned with fried chicken, homemade baked macaroni and cheese and green beans. Looking at the food she brought out, I knew why she was so angry with me. I had to make sure I brought her flowers tomorrow.

"This looks amazing honey."

"It would have been better fresh," she said.

I didn't reply to that. I knew she was still angry and I had a feeling it wasn't just about me being late.

We all began to eat passing dishes around. I occasionally slipped my son a few pieces of chicken while we ate and talked. I restarted the conversation about Kenneth and his dating situation.

"Evelyn," I said. "Do you have any single friends you could hook Ken up with?"

The perpetual frown on her face changed. She lit up at my words. She eagerly began to list a barrage of women that would "Just be so perfect for Ken!"

"My friend Karen just got a divorce and is interested in a good man. Jocelyn has three kids from a previous marriage and is looking for a good father figure…"

She went on and on about the women Kenneth should marry and start having babies with. I sat back in my seat and chuckled to myself. I listened for a few more minutes before even I couldn't take it anymore. I decided to sneak away to my office while they continued their discussion. I didn't miss the dirty look Kenneth gave me as I exited.

After Evelyn had worn herself out, Kenneth joined me in my office. I was in the midst of drinking whiskey and coke when he walked in. He plopped down in the chair in front of me.

"Don't do that again," he said taking a deep breath and letting it out. "How does she know so many people?"

I laughed before taking a sip of my drink.

"From work, church and mommy and me groups. She surprisingly interacts with a lot of people on a daily basis. Maybe you should take her up on some of those women she suggested."

He shook his head.

"Nope. Most of them seemed desperate and I'm not sure I even want kids right away. Some of these ladies come with readymade families. Plus," he said leaning back in his chair. "There is someone in my line of sight. Someone I am pursuing."

I sat my drink down on my desk and folded my arms across my chest. "Really? Tell me more."

He smiled. "Well, there is nothing official yet. I'm still courting her."

I laughed. "Courting huh?"

"Yes, I want to take it slow."

"Cool," I said. "Where did you meet her?"

I was happy to hear my brother interested in someone. Maybe this could lead somewhere.

His relationships were always a hot mess. One chick he met at a strip club and when she tried to break things off, he stalked the poor girl until the cops were called on him. He hasn't dated anyone since. Before that, he tried to save another stripper. He dated her for a few months until he found out she had a boyfriend who was spending all the money he was giving her. My hope is that he learned his lesson and this relationship will have a better outcome.

"I met her at the *Inferno*," he said not looking me in the eye.

I sighed. It seemed he was back to his old dating habits.

"Kenneth," I said calmly. I knew that if I started off yelling at him, like I wanted to, he wouldn't listen. He would only yell back and what I say would go in one ear and out the other. He could be very volatile when he wanted to be. "When are you going to listen to me? The women at the lounge are not marriage or even dating material."

"I hear you Mal, but this one is different…"

"They are all the same, Ken. They only pretend to love you and care about you as long as you continue to pay them. You've been through this before. It's like you have amnesia."

He stood.

"I told you about her because I wanted you to know I met someone. I wasn't asking you for your opinion or permission!"

He was getting angry and I knew no matter what I said he was never going to hear me. He was my little brother and I wanted to lead him in the right direction. It seemed, however, he was going to have to learn the hard way.

"Look bro, just…just don't say I didn't warn you."

He shook his head.

"You're overreacting. I'll be fine," he said pulling a peppermint from his pocket and popping it into his mouth.

My senses were ignited and I felt myself become aroused.

"You know what Ken," I began. "I have some work to do. It'll probably take me all night," I lied.

He nodded.

"No problem, I have a few things at the office I need to work on to be ready for tomorrow."

I walked my brother to the door not wanting to seem eager for him to leave. I didn't want Ken to know I really needed to get to the lounge.

Once he left, I had to spend some time listening to my wife's day, read my daughter a book, make sure my son was fast asleep and then work until my wife was in a deep sleep herself. With the house quiet, I slipped out excited to get another taste of Kim. I snuck out the house realizing in my gut I was heading for trouble but knowing   that   wasn't   enough   to   stop   me.

CHAPTER 14

Kenneth

The sun was setting and the leaves crunched under my feet as I ran. I went for a late jog to clear my head. I spent the last couple of days thinking about what my brother said to me. I heard him loud and clear. Looking for love at a strip club or a brothel was insanity. I understood this but the pull I felt toward Kim was undeniable.

I had no idea what she thought about me. When we made love there was something there. Something I hadn't experienced with another woman before. However, she was an escort and like Malcolm said, their job was to make you feel like they cared just to get what they needed…your money.

I thought maybe if I took her on a real date. If I got her out of the atmosphere of the lounge I could get a better understanding of how she truly felt.

I cut my jog short and raced back home to shower and get dressed. I intended to go to the lounge to see Kim. I was going to ask her on a date. I meant it when I said I wanted to court her. Maybe my brother was right, but I needed to see for myself.

On my way to the lounge, I stopped at a nearby late night grocery store and bought flowers…pink and white carnations. I arrived at *Inferno* on a mission. I walked inside and looked around. I didn't see Kim amongst the crowd. I headed to the bar assuming Sasha would know where Kim was. Sasha noticed as I approached and smiled.

"Hey cutie, long time no see." She noticed the carnations and grinned. "For me? You shouldn't have."

I laughed sitting the bouquet down on the counter and taking a seat on one of the stools.

"Sorry, they're for someone else."

She set down a napkin. On top of it she placed a bourbon and cola.

I looked at it and back at her. "This one won't kill me will it?"

She laughed."No, I made it just the way you like it. I even named it."

"Oh you did. What's the name?" I asked.

"The 'Bitch Cocktail'," she said laughing.

I chuckled right along with her.

"What are you doing here?" she asked. "Wendy's not here tonight."

I nodded.

"I know, but I'm not here to see Wendy."

She furrowed her brow. "Then who are you here to see?"

Just then April approached. April has been at the club about as long as Wendy and Ashley. I knew her as a loud mouth gossip. She sat down on the stool next to me.

"Sasha, can I get a double shot of vodka?" she asked. "It's been a long night."

She turned and looked at me.

"Well, look who we have here. One of the Johnson brothers."

"Hi April," I said taking a sip of my drink.

"Kenneth, Wendy is out today." April said

"I was just asking him if he finally decided to drop that bitch and find someone else to fuck," Sasha responded.

April giggled.

"Sasha that mouth of yours..." I said laughing.

"I told you," she said. "I don't hold anything back."

I folded my arms across my chest.

"Well, you happen to be right. I'm here looking for someone else."

Sasha's eyes enlarged and she stumbled backwards with her hand on her chest. "WHAT!"

"So one of the new girls caught your eye," April replied.

I raised an eyebrow. I was reluctant to say anything in front of April. She looked like she couldn't wait to hear. She was drooling over the opportunity to spread some more gossip. Despite my reservations, I continued.

"I'm looking for Kim." I pointed to the flowers. "These are for her."

The smiles on their faces disappeared. They exchanged a look of surprise then their eyes came back to me.

"Well, you need to stop looking for Kim. She doesn't need any of the problems you will bring," April responded.

I frowned.

"What are you talking about? What problems could I bring her?

I knew I had some issues in my past as far as relationships go, but I thought I was a catch. I always prided myself on treating a woman right.

"WENDY!" April and Sasha said in unison.

"She has already threatened Kim," April claimed.

"Threatened her?" I said. "What do you mean?"

That was absurd to me. It wasn't like Wendy was my girlfriend or something. She had plenty of clients and it wasn't like I was her best paying client either.

"She told Kim if she tried to steal her any of her clients away, she would make her life a living hell," April responded.

"And you know she could," Sasha added.

Malcolm was right. This place was shit. Kim didn't deserve to be threatened by anyone. What we had was far beyond this shit hole. As soon as I made her see that, hopefully I could convince her to leave. In the meantime, I knew I had to do something about Wendy...

"I can handle Wendy," I reassured them.

"Ha!" Sasha said. "You brothers!"

"What is that suppose to mean?" I asked.

"Nothing," she said shaking her head. She walked away to serve another patron.

April took her vodka and downed the double shot. Then she brought her attention back to me.

We had no clue someone else was listening to our conversation.

"There are plenty of other new girls here. Why don't you request one of them?" she asked.

I opened my mouth to answer but was interrupted by our eavesdropper.

"He may need to request someone else anyway," a voice said from behind me.

I turned to find Luciano standing there.

"Why can't he request Kim?" Sasha asked coming back over to join us.

"Well, a VIP already requested her and asked if she could solely be his. Tony approved it."

"What?" we all said at the same time.

I knew how the requesting process went. If someone asked Tony for her that meant she could only be with that person. I hated that process. It meant I couldn't request to see her. How was I going to court her if I wasn't allowed to be with her? I knew I had to get creative. I was going to have to regroup and make sure I convinced Kim, this place was beneath her.

"If you see Kim, give her these," I said pointing toward the flowers.

Then I stood and walked toward the exit more determined than ever to win her heart.

CHAPTER 15

Kimberly

I could barely breathe but I didn't say anything. I didn't want to ruin the moment. I was so close to coming. I didn't want him to stop. My hips rocked back and forth as I rode his dick. His hand squeezed my throat while the other gripped my ass.

"Grind on that dick, baby," he demanded.

His words were the last straw. I went over the edge and came hard with him inside of me. It was difficult to keep riding him after my orgasm. He could tell so he flipped me over onto my back. He pulled my legs apart. The power I felt when he flipped me and pulled my legs…scared me. I had never been handled so forcefully by anyone before.

The way he fucked me was more than just rough sex. It seemed like he got a kick out of being rough and inflicting pain on me. It frightened me more that it turned me on. I knew I should just get my shit and run whenever he came to see me, but deep down…I liked it. He made me come harder than I had ever come before and I secretly yearned to be in bed with him.

He entered me forcefully yanking my legs up and placing them on either shoulder. I could feel him deeper. I grabbed a hold of the sheets embracing the pleasure and the pain. I moaned loudly placing my hand on his chest. He dropped one leg and continued to pound me. The friction on my clit was just too much to handle and I came again with a shriek.

"That's right baby scream. Let me know how much you like it," he said still going and not letting up on his aggressive pace.

Suddenly his hand was around my neck again squeezing as he came. He collapsed on the bed next to me. He lay that way for a second before he finally rose and climbed off. I watched as he discarded the used condom in the waste basket.

He came back over to me and lay on a pillow.

"You are fucking amazing!" he said. "Damn! You earned every dollar and then some."

I smiled.

"I don't know if I've ever been called amazing so much," I said rolling onto my stomach.

"Well get used to it," he said slapping me on the ass.

"Ouch!" I exclaimed.

"Oh, you're going to have to up your tolerance for pain. There are much harsher punishments where that came from. I have been going easy on you so far."

I thought about the choking and the pain he loved to inflict and thought, *that wasn't the worse he could do?"* That worried me a little.

"Malcolm, why do you have to choke me whenever we fuck?"

He laughed. I was perplexed.

"Why are you laughing? What's so funny?" I asked.

"Just hearing that word come out of your pretty little mouth makes me laugh. It's not natural for you."

"What word? Fuck?"

He laughed even harder.

"Yes," he answered. "You seem so innocent and hearing you say that word is weird."

"I say 'fuck' all the time." I didn't see the big deal.

He smiled seductively. Then he reached out and grabbed my face in his hands. He brought his face to mine.

"Say it again."

I looked into his eyes.

"Fuck…"

"Hearing you say it turns me on,"

He pulled me by my face toward his and kissed me. His tongue played with mine. I rubbed my hands up and down his arms. I pulled back when I felt marks there.

"Where did you get these scratches?" I asked.

He let me go and set up. He climbed off the bed and began to put his clothes back on.

"My kids just got a new cat. It scratched me."

I joined him and began to put my clothes back on.

"I would bend you over and fuck you from behind, but it's late and I need to get home to my wife and kids."

At that moment it really hit me. He had a wife at home. There was a woman out there who loved him and was waiting for him. The mother of his children was waiting… Guilt began to set in and I finished putting on my clothes.

"You're right. It's late you should get home. I'm going to head home too. Have a good night." I said heading toward the door.

"You're forgetting something," he said.

I turned and saw him standing there holding a stack of bills in his hands. I could tell the money was more than what he owed me. I walked over and grabbed it from him. I began to count it.

"What? You don't trust me or something?" he asked.

He gave me $1,000 more than he owed me. I handed it back to him. He shook his head.

"No, keep it. I know you have school and probably need to pay rent and things like that. Just call it a tip."

I looked at him.

"Maybe you could put this in your kids' school fund instead of spending it on me."

The smiled wiped off his face and he reached out grabbing me. He gripped my face again and pulled me close to him.

"My family is fucking off limits to you as well as what I do with my money."

He snatched the $1,000 out of my hand and put it in his pocket while still holding on to me. I had no experience with a violent man and I was afraid of him. He finally let me go with a push. I stumbled backward but was able to balance myself and not fall flat on my back.

I didn't say another word to him. I was shocked by his violence. I had hoped that his aggression was only during sex but I could tell that it went much further than that. I wondered if Ashley had to put up with this. I stuffed the rest of the bills I had into the pocket of my robe and left the room.

As I exited I ran into April in the hallway.

"I've been looking all over for you," she said.

"Me? Why?"

She opened her mouth to speak then closed it. She noticed what I was wearing and my disheveled appearance.

"Were you with a client?" she asked.

"Yes," I answered. "What's going on and why were you looking for me?"

"Why is Kenneth Johnson bringing you flowers? I told you to stay away from the Johnson brothers."

I raised my eyebrows in surprise.

"Well, he told me he wanted to court me. He said he didn't want just a sexual relationship with me here. He wanted more. I just thought he was joking…"

"Well apparently he wasn't," she said.

I couldn't help myself. I smiled a little. I didn't realize he was serious. Men say lots of things in this place, but bringing me flowers? I had never had a man bring me flowers. It made me feel warm all over.

"Oh don't look so happy. What's going to happen when Wendy finds out?"

Hearing Wendy's name ruined the moment. I rolled my eyes. Why was everyone so afraid of Wendy? She was this itty bitty woman that threatened a lot of action but I had yet to see any.

"April, please," I said. "I'm so sick of hearing about Wendy. I could care less. I'm not going to let her run me like she does you guys."

"You have no idea," she said hands on her hips. "You've been here for five months and all of a sudden you think you know everything."

I sighed and let my eyes travel up toward the ceiling.

"Look at me, little girl. You don't want Wendy as an enemy."

Just then the door behind me opened and out came Malcolm. April's eyes grew larger and I sighed. I knew there would be more yelling at me over this.

"Ladies," he said with a huge smile on his face. "What are we doing? Having a mini party in the hallway?"

April glared at him.

"Malcolm, have a good night. Go home to your family," she said pointing down the hall toward the stairs.

"Okay, April," he chuckled. Then he reached over and grabbed me pulling me toward him. He kissed me passionately then let me go. He slid past me down the hall.

When he was gone, she turned on me. "What are you trying to do?"

"I'm trying to stay safe and take advantage of my luck."

"What does that even mean?" she asked. She didn't wait for me to reply before she laid into me. "You want to stay safe? You don't want to follow the rules? You ain't been here long enough to try and change things. You haven't paid dues."

I knew where she was coming from. For years they have been doing things a certain way. It was hard to accept change and a new regime. I wasn't saying that I was here to shake things up, but I didn't plan to be pushed around. If I was going to do this to further my education, I was going to do things my way, on my terms.

"Look April," I began. "I am lucky. I do not have some creepy greasy guys trying to sleep with me. I've seen some of your clients. Why should we give Wendy and Ashley monopoly over these guys? Why do you have to take whatever you can get while they get to see whomever they please?"

She flared her nostrils and let out a stream of air. I took a step toward her.

"Plus we need to be smart here," I said placing my hand on her shoulder. "We need to be with guys that we trust. Sarah is dead because of a client she had. No one else needs to end up like her. Malcolm is my ticket to staying safe."

I could tell she didn't like what I had to say. She turned her back on me. I just stood there staring at her. Then she finally turned around to face me.

"Okay, Kim. You think you know everything. I see you have to learn the hard way." She slid her hands against each other. "I wash my hands of this. You can go and take your pretty carnations home and have sex with both brothers. I don't care anymore." She walked away from me down the hall and descended the stairs. I leaned against the wall and thought to myself,

He   bought   me   carnations.   I   love   carnations.

CHAPTER 16

Kimberly

"Uh oh, here comes trouble," Sasha said as I took a seat at the bar.

"Very funny," I laughed. "I didn't come here to start problems."

It had been a couple of days since April chewed me out for being involved with Kenneth and Malcolm. Since then, she has barely said two words to me. I couldn't completely understand why she was so upset. I was hoping Sasha could shed some light on the situation.

"Well, for someone who isn't looking to start shit around here, you sure have landed in a lot of it."

I sighed.

She was right. I may have gotten a little cocky and ahead of myself. I'd been running my mouth an awful lot lately. Yet I felt that I had some justification for it.

"Sasha," I began. "It's not my fault. I was requested by Malcolm and Kenneth. It's not like I have a huge say in the matter."

"True," she replied. "But you could have handled things better with April. You totally disrespected her."

I raised an eyebrow.

"How? I was just being honest with her. Like I said, it wasn't…"

"Your fault," she interrupted. "I hear you, Kim. Yet the way you talked to her, telling her she's allowing Ashley and Wendy to run her and give her the nasty sleazy clients really hit a nerve."

I took a deep breath and exhaled. I knew I was going to have to apologize to April. She had done nothing but try to help me and I threw it in her face. I'm glad I consulted Sasha about this. I knew she would help me put things into perspective.

"With all that being said…" Sasha said "You've got some balls girl. I like that!"

I laughed. "I thought you didn't like balls."

She roared with laughter and walked away from me to service another customer. Suddenly someone grabbed the barstool next to me and took a seat. I turned and found myself face to face with Kenneth.

"Hello beautiful," he said.

I smiled.

"Well, hello," I replied. "What can I do for you?"

He smiled.

"Did you get my flowers?"

I nodded.

"How did you know carnations were my favorite?"

He reached on the side of him and grabbed a box sitting on the counter. He slid it over to me. I looked over at him and giggled.

"You bought me chocolates?"

"Yes," he said. "You seem like a girl that likes chocolates."

"You were serious about this courting me thing, huh?" I asked letting my fingers trail the outline of the box.

"I'm serious about taking you out and showing you a good time."

I shook my head. "I'm not sure that's a good idea."

He cocked his head to the side. "What could it hurt, sweetheart? Dinner, a movie…"

I sighed.

Kenneth seemed like a really nice guy and that was the problem. Working as an escort, the last thing I needed was a nice guy. It didn't help that I was being paid to sleep with his brother…who was married. I had no clue if he knew any of that. What I did know was a relationship with Kenneth would never work.

"I'm sorry but I have to decline." I said pushing the chocolates back over to him.

He leaned in close sliding the box back over to me.

"I just want to let you know. I am very persistent," he said. "I don't give up very easy."

I leaned in myself bringing our lips so close together. One more inch. I could almost taste him.

"The answer will always be no," I replied.

He smiled.

"We'll see about that." Then he kissed me gently on the lips. He pulled back and I opened my eyes. *When had I closed them?* He grinned from ear to ear. I could tell he knew the affect he had on me. There were butterflies in my stomach for the first time in years. I stared into his brown eyes and was lost.

It was at that moment I heard a yell.

"KIM!"

I sat up and looked over to see my worst nightmare walking toward me. I knew this confrontation was going to happen. April told me so. I just didn't prepare for it to happen tonight.

Wendy approached Kenneth and I with her hands on her wide hips.

"I see I caught you in the act even after I warned you."

Kenneth stood and opened his mouth to speak, but I stopped him by placing a hand on his chest. I didn't need any help. I had to handle this myself.

"What am I doing that has your panties in a bunch?" I asked standing and folding my arms across my chest.

"Please," she said. "You know what you're doing. Trying to steal my client." She took a step toward me.

I looked around to see there were quite a few people watching us. That made me a little bolder and mouthier.

"I don't have to steal your clients. In your old age, they're just leaving."

As the words left my mouth I knew it was probably too much. But I had already said it.

Couldn't take it back now.

There were a few snickers at my comment. Kenneth tried to get between us but I stepped in front of him bringing myself closer to Wendy. That may have been a mistake.

"Bitch! I thought I made myself clear. Stay away from Kenneth or I'm going to fuck you up."

"Wendy, enough..." Kenneth began but again I stopped him.

"Wendy, I'm not afraid of you," I responded.

At my words, the room went silent. I was sure now everyone was involved in my conversation. I swallowed the lump in my throat. My heart pounded.

I took a step back.

"You're not afraid?" she chuckled. "Well, you should be. You need to learn your place in this business and stealing clients will get your head busted open." She poked me in the chest after her statement.

I knew with eyes on me I couldn't back down. I looked and saw Sasha. She was shaking her head and mouthing the word "No." It was too late now. I had to put my money where my mouth was. I wasn't going to let her intimidate me like she and Ashley tried to do before. I wouldn't be embarrassed again.

"Whatever, Wendy," I replied. "The ancient rules you and your crony put into place are done." I said poking her back.

It was like poking a sleeping bear. I saw her fist clinch at her side and I took another step back.

She surprised me by laughing.

"You've been here a few months and now you think you make the rules? Bitch, please!"

"You're right. I don't make the rules. The men in this club do. Too bad they don't want you." I said. I held up my index and middle finger. "Peace! Good luck being too old to matter."

I turned to walk away. I felt a hand on my shoulder. I thought it was Kenneth so I turned around. A fist hit me square in the jaw. I stumbled backward, lost my balance and landed hard on my butt. Before I had a chance to understand what just happened, Wendy had me pinned to the floor throwing more punches.

I could only defend myself placing my forearms in front of my face. When the opportunity arose I scratched at her face hoping it would make her back off. It only made her angrier as she straddled me. Finally someone pulled her off and I was raised from the floor. Kenneth pulled me into his arms as I was in a daze.

She continued to scream calling me all kinds of names.

"You better hide bitch because I'm not done with you," she screamed.

Luciano, who pulled her off me, led her upstairs and away from the crowd that gathered to see the pandemonium.

"Are you okay?" Kenneth asked me. He gently touched my face. I could tell it was already starting to swell.

"No, I'm not okay." I said.

I was angry, humiliated and just needed to get out of there. Sasha was over by me now also checking my face. I fanned her hands away.

She looked up at Kenneth with wild eyes.

"I thought you were going to handle Wendy," she said.

He sighed and went upstairs after her. I was happy he left. I didn't want him to see me cry.

"Kim," Sasha began, but I didn't let her finish. I grabbed my purse from the counter and ran out of the lounge not sure if I would ever return.

CHAPTER 17

"That bitch scratched my face!" Wendy said staring into the mirror.

I sat on the bed with a first aid kit in my lap.

"If you would stop picking at it and let me help you, I can make sure it won't leave a scar," I said tapping my fingers impatiently on the box containing the first aid items.

"I can handle this," she said holding a tissue to her face. "What are her nails made of? Razor blades?"

I laughed.

"This is not funny. These new bitches think they can just walk into this place and work on other people's clients," she ranted. "Uh NO! Not on my watch."

"Wendy come sit down. I'll clean you up," I insisted.

She stomped her way in bare feet over to where I sat on the bed. She plopped down next to me. I placed my hand on her chin and brought her head around to face me. I examined her wound.

"These are really deep scratches. She got you really good," I said.

I opened up the kit and pulled out some cotton balls and rubbing alcohol wipes.

"That's going to burn. Don't use that," she whined.

"Wendy, I have to clean you up."

She took a deep breath and I applied the wipes. She winced and grabbed my hand.

"No, never mind. It hurts."

I smiled and shook my head.

"Look, I'll get you a drink. It will help you to calm down and forget about the pain."

"Fine," she said folding her arms across her chest.

I stood and sat the kit down on the bed. I walked over to the wet bar in the room and began to mix her a drink. I had gotten very good at this lately. I knew just the perfect drink to mask the drugs I dumped into the glass. I made a cocktail of cherry vodka, grenadine, lime juice and sprite. I walked back over and handed her the mixture. I sat down next to her. She drank half of it and placed the rest down on the floor next to her foot.

"I've been working here for 16 years and I get no respect anymore. I may be older but I can still pull a man without a problem," she said.

"I agree. You have become more beautiful with age," I said looking down at the half empty glass sitting by her feet.

"These young women walk in here and think they can just do away with the hierarchy in this place. They can't just waltz in here and take our clients."

She looked down.

"Wendy, are you okay?" I asked.

She looked back up and I saw tears in her eyes.

"Who am I kidding?" she began. "I'm getting older. There are only so many clients I can get now. I get the old men that are balding or have kids the ages of the girls out there. How am I supposed to compete anymore?"

My heart went out to Wendy. Tony has been hiring them younger and younger. Some of the girls, like Kim, are still in their early twenties. When you are in your mid to late thirties, in this business, those girls are a major threat. That's why she and Ashley invented this hierarchy Tony didn't even enforce. Through intimidation and threats of violence, they had convinced the rest of the girls and a few men that they have power they don't really have.

I reached down and grabbed the glass. Swishing it around a little, I handed the drink to Wendy.

"Drink up. This will make you feel better."

She shook her head.

"No. What will make me feel better is if I can beat Kim's ass some more."

I laughed.

"I promise you. Drink this and you will relax and feel better."

She took the glass and looked at the alcohol inside. Then she looked up at me suspiciously. She looked at the glass again.

"You put something in this didn't you?"

I felt panicked. My heart rate increased. I had to think quickly.

"Yes, just a little bit of Xanax. It'll calm you down," I confessed. I knew by telling her the truth I may risk her not drinking it.

She smiled.

"Why didn't you say so?" she said. "Abigail was my supplier and I hadn't been able to get anymore for a while."

I watched as she devoured the rest of the drink. She stood still holding the glass. She walked around the bed and set the glass on the side table next to the bed.

"You can be my supplier now," she informed me.

She walked back over to the end of the bed.

"You're right. I can feel it already. I feel good," she confessed.

I raised an eyebrow. This was not what I had in mind. I needed her to pass out. My body was aching to feel that thrill again. It had been too long since I felt that power, that exhilarating feeling. I saw Wendy as my opportunity to get it. I stood and approached her. I wrapped my arms around her waist.

"Come over here and lay down."

"No, I feel so good," she said.

Suddenly her knees buckled and I caught her. I led her back to the bed. She was wearing a black strapless dress and it slide down exposing her breast somewhat. I licked my lips. Her 5'1'' frame was thick and sexy. I didn't care how old she was. She turned me on.

I was successfully able to get her to lie down on the bed. She lay with her legs dangling a little off the edge. Her eyes were closed and she had a smile on her face.

"I know how to make you feel even better," I said sliding her dress up her smooth caramel colored legs.

"Mmmm," she moaned eyes still closed. She scooted herself further on the bed so that her legs no longer dangled.

I let my hand travel up her body until I reached a tangle of hair between her thighs. She wasn't wearing any panties. I continued and she didn't stop me. I pulled her dress up until her pussy came into view. I spread her legs and dropped my head. I took a deep inhale of her musky scent. I reached out my tongue and tasted her. She stirred a little but she wasn't fighting me. She was enjoying herself.

I didn't want her to enjoy herself. After my encounter with Sarah, this was not enough for me. The experience I had with Sarah spoiled me. I needed that feeling again and I needed it now.

I ate her some more until I had my fill, then I straddled her. She finally opened her eyes.

"What…What are you doing," she asked.

I didn't reply. I just continued to explore her body with my hands.

"Get…get off me." Her words came out slow and slurred.

I didn't do as she requested. I continued to straddle her and squeeze her breasts. She began to buck to throw me off. It only made me smile.

There we go! Let's fight!

I immediately wrapped my fingers around her neck. She began to buck harder, but I held on squeezing. I could feel my body respond to the sensation. I held her life in my hands and I felt exhilarated. My cock hardened and I began to sweat. I was suddenly warm all over.

She struggled and fought but I knew she had more than just Xanax in her system. There was a large amount of sleeping pills included. Eventually she would pass out and I would be free to conquer her. That seemed to be taking awhile longer than I hoped. I gripped her neck tighter and tighter.

She struggled and pulled at my hands trying to free herself. Her brown eyes were wild. Her arms stretched out and unbeknownst to me she was close enough to the side table to reach for some help. It came without a warning. She grabbed the drinking glass from the table and smashed it against the side of my face. The glass cracked and cut me on the side of the head. I let her go and grabbed for my face. When I pulled it away there was blood.

She used the opportunity in my dazed state to get away from me and off the bed. When I finally noticed she was no longer underneath me, she was halfway to the door crawling. I leaped off the bed. I grabbed her just before she reached the door.

"Help!" she screamed loud enough for others to hear.

The last thing I needed was for someone to come in here before I had a chance to finish.

I needed to finish.

"Help!" she screamed again.

I straddled her back and put my forearm across her neck. It wasn't difficult. The drugs were finally fully kicking in and she could no longer fight. I pulled her into a choke hold maneuver and squeezed. I felt my cock grow and harden as she went unconscious. I knew I needed more than that. I continued to squeeze knowing from experience it took at least three minutes before it would be official.

I moaned feeling myself almost burst from my pants. I felt her go completely limp and I released. Her head fell forward as I moved. I needed to take advantage of this moment. I undid the button and the zipper on my pants. I pulled out my member and began to stroke it. I sat on my heels next to her body and I stroked it hard and furiously until I erupted all over my hands. It felt so good I wanted to cry. I sat there trying to regain my composure.

Suddenly she stirred.

She wasn't dead.

I took a deep breath. I was bleeding from my head, I had cum all over my hands and she wasn't dead.

It was going to take me a little longer to clean up this scene.

I had work to do...

CHAPTER 18

Malcolm

There was a silver lining to the death of Wendy. Her body was found early in the morning when all the girls were gone and the only ones there was the cleaning crew. By the time the police arrived there wasn't very many people left to question.

Inferno was now a crime scene…again. That meant I once again had to deal with an angry ranting Tony Santino.

He called me at 5am to tell me about Wendy's demise. Apparently the cleaning crew was so freaked out about finding a dead body they called the police instead of calling him first. Once I found out, I immediately mobilized attorneys from our firm to head over to help in case any legal issues would arise.

That didn't sit well with Tony.

"Where the fuck are you, Malcolm?" he yelled through the phone.

"I'll be there soon. I need to head to the office first, then I'll head your way," I lied.

The truth is I just wasn't ready to face all the bullshit with the cops and Tony. I also wasn't prepared to deal with another dead woman.

"I'm your fucking priority Malcolm. Get your ass down here," he said ending the call.

I didn't appreciate the way he talked to me. He was just one client out of many at our firm. I was not his slave. Plus the other attorneys were more than capable of handling this without my help.

I decided to wait a little longer before I headed over. The longer I waited the more my phone rang. It continued to ring over and over again. I didn't have to check. I knew it was Tony. I'd deal with him when I was good and ready.

I spun around in my chair and tried to focus on the sights outside of my office window. It was actually a beautiful fall morning. The sun was out and the trees still had leaves of brown, red and yellow.

The outside was overshadowed by my phone. When the ringing stopped, not long after, it would begin to ring again.

I ignored it.

"Aren't you going to answer that?" I heard from behind me.

I turned in my chair to find Kenneth leaning against the door frame. I hadn't heard my door open I was so lost in my thoughts.

I raised an eyebrow.

"What are you doing here?" I asked.

Before he could reply, I noticed the bloody gash on the side of his head. It was covered in gauze and bandages, yet you could still see the blood soaking through.

"What the hell happened to you?"

His hand moved up to lightly touch the wound. He flinched.

"Oh this?" he said. "I fell out of bed this morning,"

He chuckled. "I hit my head on my side table."

"You really got yourself good," I responded.

"Yeah," he said walking over to take a seat in the chair in front of my desk.

"Why aren't you at the lounge?" he asked.

"I had a few things to follow up on first," I replied still focusing on the cut on his head. "Maybe you should go to the hospital."

He shook his head.

"NO!" he exclaimed.

I narrowed my eyes at him.

"No," he said in a calmer voice. "I'm fine."

"Okay," I said raising my hands in surrender.

My phone began to ring again. I picked it up to make sure it was Tony before I rejected the call.

"Are you just going to keep ignoring him? You know it only makes him throw a tantrum." Kenneth said.

I sighed. He was right. The angrier Tony was the worse it was going to be.

I stood.

"You're right," I said grabbing my phone and put it in my pocket. I snatched up my car keys and my suit jacket. "I'm just going to head over now."

Kenneth stood as well and followed me out of my office and down the hall to the elevators. When we reached them I pushed the down button and waited.

"I take it you heard what's going on?"

He nodded.

"When you stopped answering your phone, Tony began to call me. He told me everything. It's such a shame that anyone could...hurt a woman like that."

I sighed.

"I'm not shocked. Wendy was a nasty bitch," I replied. "I'm glad you came here instead of going down there. I don't need you caught up in this mess again."

I looked over at Kenneth and realized he was quiet all of a sudden. He was sneaking glances at me while we waited.

"You got something to say to me little brother?" I questioned just as the elevator dinged and the doors slid opened. The cab was empty so we walked inside. I pressed the button for the parking garage and leaned against the wall.   When the doors closed, Kenneth spoke.

"Malcolm, I was at the club last night."

I turned to him and heaved a sigh trying to calm down before I spoke.

"Ken…"

"I know what you're going to say. There is no need to lecture me."

I raised an eyebrow. "Really? Then why do you just continue to ignore everything I tell you. Why can't you stay away from those girls? You know they're only going to bring you trouble. You've been around for three murders now. How is that going to look?"

"Malcolm, you're overreacting. Plus, it's my life. You may have the perfect married life and the perfect family but I don't, okay?

The elevator door opened and people from another floor entered. It took everything I had not to continue to yell at him. It's one thing to play around with these girls once in a while, but to fall for them over and over…

The doors opened again and all the people exited on the first floor. After they were gone, the doors closed and we headed down to the parking garage.

"So you've decided to frequent the club and now you're a witness. I hope the bitch you're seeing is worth it. Someone is going to let it slip that you were there and then you'll be caught. You keep getting jammed up at *Inferno* and you could lose your job."

The doors opened and we walked out. I followed Kenneth to his car.

"The last thing I want to do is lecture you. You're you a grown man. I shouldn't have to tell you unless you're working for the Santinos, you shouldn't be anywhere near that lounge."

He stopped walking and turned to face me.

"Why do you work for them anyway?" he asked. "You have other big time clients, yet you spend all your time at the club pacifying Tony. Why?"

My brother had no clue how powerful the Santino family was in this city. The amount of dirt they had on judges, police officers, the district attorney's office and public officials was insurmountable. My senior partner happened to be one of the people Antonio Santino Sr. was holding hostage with information.

"Look, it's complicated. Trust me. Just stay away."

We reached his car and he pressed the button on his keys. The car beeped to signal it was now unlocked.

"Hey, I need to go. We'll have to finish this later. You should come over for dinner," I said.

I reached up to touch the wound on his head.

"But first, you should see a doctor."

He smiled.

"Alright, I'll see a doctor," he said before he climbed into his car.

I turned and walked to my car with my phone starting to ring again. I pulled it out and saw it wasn't Tony calling me. Luciano was.

Reluctantly, I answered.

"Malcolm, we need you down here. I heard someone mention a serial killer and Tony is flipping out. We need you!"

"I'm on my way Luc," I informed him.

I didn't pull off right away. I sat in the car for a few more minutes.

I wasn't ready to enter the fray.

CHAPTER 19

Kenneth

"Where is my client?" I asked Detective Marshall.

He stood with his arms folded across his chest with a smug smile across his face.

"We have her upstairs," he said. "She's fine. We've taken good care of her."

Then he pointed to my head.

"What happened to you?" he asked.

I reached up to touch the tender spot. It was still painful two days later. I left the urgent care last night with six stitches, medication for the pain and antibiotics to keep infection at bay.

"It was an accident. Now, take me to my client." I ordered.

He sighed and moved toward the elevators. I followed trying to calm down and retain some form of professionalism.

I received a call from Luciano early this morning. He said the security guards told the police about Kim's fight with Wendy. Now that Wendy was dead they were interested in speaking to her. April called Luciano when the cops came by. They insisted she come downtown with them and talk. I was furious. I wasted no time getting dressed and rushed to get her.

The elevator doors opened and we walked inside. He pressed the button for the third floor. The doors closed and we were alone.

"This is all over, you know? Now that her attorney is here."

He chuckled.

"For you to be her lawyer, she doesn't seem to need your help. She didn't ask for you once."

I side-eyed him, and then continued to look straight ahead. I wasn't going to react to this cop's dig. I was focused on getting Kim out of here.

The elevator doors opened and we entered a room bustling with energy. Phones were ringing, people were everywhere and no one seemed to notice I was even there. It was pure chaos. I almost bumped into a woman carrying a stack of papers. She didn't even stop.

The police station was an old abandoned hospital that was renovated to fit the police department's needs. They did as little work as possible as the lobby and most of the rooms still looked like a dusty medical facility. Hallways and rolls of rooms that used to hold sick and/or dying patients now held offices for lieutenants, sergeants and interrogations. I spent many a time here picking up my clients or sitting in on line-ups that could implicate those I was tasked to defend.

I followed Detective Marshall through the madness to the back. We went through a set of double doors and down a long hallway.

When we reached the end, Marshall stopped at a room to the right.

"Your client is in there."

I opened the door to find Kim sitting on one side of a wooden table and two other detectives sat across from her. She had a glass of water and a gray blanket covering her shoulders. I had no clue what they had already discussed but I hoped Kim was smart enough not to say a word.

When she saw me her eyes widened.

"Kenneth?" she said.

I could tell she'd been crying. Dried tear marks slid down her face and her eyes were bloodshot. I approached and kneeled down in front of her.

"Are you alright?" I asked.

Her right eye was slightly swollen from her fight with Wendy and had developed a dark ring around it.

She nodded.

I could tell she had the same concern for me. Her eyes fell on the wound on my head.

"What happened?" she asked. "Are you okay?"

She reached up as if to touch the injury but instead let her fingers hover near it.

"It's a long story." I replied.

Standing, I turned to the detectives.

"This ends now!" I said "She's not saying another word."

"Whoa," one of the other detectives said standing."She's free to go. We don't have her under arrest or anything...yet."

"Come on Kim," I said removing the blanket from her. "I'm getting you out of here."

She didn't say another word. She just grabbed my hand and I led her out of the room.

"I wouldn't plan trips out of town any time soon, Miss Lawson," Detective Marshall yelled at us. I continued to walk down the hall holding her hand. It wasn't lost on me how the sensation of her skin so close to mine made me feel.

The ride back to her house was quiet. She stared out of the window the entire time. I wanted to speak to her but I could tell she was still shook up. Being interrogated most of the morning by police can do that to you. An instinct to protect her kicked in and I knew that I would be there for her through this mess.

When we reached her home, I wanted to walk her to the front door. I parked the car and stepped out in the fresh autumn air. I went around car for her but she was already out and halfway up the sidewalk. I jogged to catch up.

She pulled her keys from her purse and reached to unlock her door until she saw me there.

"What are you doing?" she asked.

I leaned against the door frame.

"Being a gentleman. Plus I could use a cup of coffee."

She raised an eyebrow and placed one hand on her hip. "So now you're coming in?"

I nodded.

"I don't think so," she said.

"Don't I at least deserve a cup of coffee and some conversation after I rescued you from the police?"

"Rescued me?" she laughed. "I had things handled."

It was my turn to laugh.

"If you had it handled you would have called your attorney before you ended up in an interrogation room. Luciano had to call me."

She studied me for a minute with her eyes narrowed. Then she smiled. She unlocked her front door.

"Come on in," she said holding the door opened for me.

I was taken aback when I entered. The house, on the inside, was covered in a gold and teal blue. The carpet, walls and every piece of furniture was touched by the colors. There was also a large China cabinet with gold-plated elephants.

"April is an impeccable decorator, huh?" Kim said giggling.

I followed her into the kitchen. I watched her go through cabinets until she had what she needed to make coffee. I gazed at her mesmerized by her beautiful body and how gorgeous she was without makeup or any other garment they wore down at the lounge. I also noticed that through her smiles and laughs she was hurting. Her shoulders slumped and when she wasn't smiling she seemed to be close to tears.

"Kim, are you alright?" I asked leaning against the counter.

She turned.

"No, I'm not alright." She folded her arms across her chest. "First, I was humiliated the other night by Wendy. My face is all battered and bruised. Then Wendy is killed and according to the police I'm a 'person of interest.' No, I'm not okay and I rather not talk about it anymore."

I sighed. I knew this looked bad but I was sure the police would back off once they figured out Kim could not have done anything to Wendy. In the meantime, I understood why she wouldn't want to talk about it.

"I'm your attorney. You're going to need to talk about it with me sometime."

She sighed.

"I understand that, but please…not right now."

She filled the coffee pot with water and poured it into the back of the coffee maker.

"Okay, we don't have to talk about it. Let's change the subject. We can chat about what time we are having dinner tonight."

"Dinner?" she said turning to face me. "Look at my face. I am not going out looking like this."

I did look at her face.

Through the bruises, I saw the most stunning woman I had ever seen.

"You're beautiful," I replied.

She squinted her eyes at me. Then she smiled.

"You're making this so hard for me," she mumbled.

She poured coffee into two mugs "Cream and sugar?" she asked pouring creamer in one cup.

"I take it black," I responded.

She handed me a mug and walked over to the large wooden table in the kitchen. I followed and took a seat next to hers.

"I don't want to make it hard. I want to make it easy. I just want you to give me a chance."

She took a sip of coffee and sighed.

"It's just not a good idea, Kenneth."

"I don't get why you won't let me just take you out. I don't want to brag but I'm a pretty good time."

She laughed. "I don't doubt that, but you're my lawyer and a client. It's just business between us."

I cocked my head to the side.

"Well, I don't have to be a client at the lounge and I can find you another excellent attorney."

She pushed her coffee cup to the side and rested her elbow on the table. She placed her head in her hand. "You think that will change my mind?"

"Yes," I said scooting my chair closer to hers. I slid my hand on top of her hand. "Without those obstacles in our way, we will have nothing but unbridled and unadulterated pleasure between us."

I leaned in closer until our lips were only inches apart. I whispered against her mouth. "I want to feel that pleasure with you."

Then I kissed her.

She pulled back. Her eyes closed then reopened. She sighed.

"Do you want me to stop?" I asked.

"No," she said. "Please, don't stop."

I grabbed her hand and pulled her over until she was in my lap, straddling me. We kissed again except this time it was hungry and primal. The need for her body and her lips against mine was something I had never felt before.

She wrapped her arms around my neck and we continued to kiss. I didn't know how much more I could take as her tongue played with mine. Her body slowly began to grind against me threatening to send me over the edge. I broke away from our kiss.

"God, girl," I said breathlessly. "You turn me on so much."

She moved from my lap to stand. She pulled down her pants moving deliberately to turn me on further. She slid them down her thighs to her ankles. It was then I realized she wasn't wearing any panties.

She kicked her pants to the side and I grabbed her and pulled her back over to me. I used my hands to push open her thighs. I dipped my head between her legs and let my tongue taste her. She moaned in reply and I continued my exploration of her sex.

She took a step back and I sat up.

"What…I," I began.

"Do you have a condom?" she asked.

I fumbled around in my pocket and pulled out my wallet. I grabbed the condom I had tucked inside and handed it to her.

I was so hard at this point. I almost came when she undid my belt. She unbuttoned and unzipped my pants. I was wearing boxers so it was easy for her to release me.

I thought she was going to take me into her mouth but she proceeded to put the condom on me instead. When she was done, she straddled me again taking her time to ease me inside of her. I groaned as her tight walls wrapped around me.

She began to grind, slow at first and as her need increased she intensified her pace. I grabbed her ass and squeezed. We moaned together until I couldn't take it anymore. Her eyes caught mine. We gazed at each other while she fucked me.

"Climb on the table," I said.

She didn't hesitate. She moved off me and moved dishes out of the way before she climbed onto the large wooden table. I stood pulling my pants and underwear down. She scooted down to give me better access. I slid inside of her and we both moaned in unison. I fucked her with fervor. It was unlike anything I'd felt before. I leaned down and we kissed. Still tasting her soft and delectable lips I felt her come. She broke from the kiss to cry out as her body tensed and then released.

"Oh, shit," she screamed.

Hearing her sparked my eruption and I came hard. I rode the wave until my knees buckled and I ended up sitting back in the chair.

"April is going to kill me," she said.

"Let me handle April," I said.

We sat in silence for a minute soaking in what just happened. Finally I spoke..

"So, dinner at seven?"

She laughed.

CHAPTER 20

Kimberly

I pulled my knees up to my chest. I didn't care I was wearing a dress. I just wanted to curl up in a ball and dream about being someplace else. I was hiding out in one of the VIP rooms that hadn't been spoiled by the death of anyone.

It had been three weeks and I was still reeling from the humiliation I received at the hand of Wendy. The lounge was back open and the police were no longer looking at me. Everyone saw me leave that night so the police had to clear me.

That knowledge still hadn't helped my mood or improve my desire to work at *Inferno*. Luciano called and begged me to return. I refused. That was when I received a call from Tony. He calmly threatened to make my life a living hell if I didn't come back. Girls don't quit when they are in demand. Malcolm wanted me so I needed to stay. I was afraid of Tony. So, I was at the lounge hiding and lamenting my current state.

I squeezed my eyes tighter when I heard the door open. I dipped my head down against my knees.

"Are you going to hide out here forever?"

It was April.

I opened my eyes and rolled over. I looked at her. Even in the dark I could see she was decked out in a shimmering gold dress with heels to match. I knew she didn't have a client tonight. It was the only time she would go all out like this. The nights she didn't have a client were the nights she needed to pull in a new one.

"I just might," I replied.

She shook her head and sat down next to me.

"Well, you need to suck it up. Wendy, rest in peace, is gone and most of the people here aren't worried about that fight. Plus…your client is here."

She rolled her eyes as she said that last line. I knew she was still upset about me seeing Malcolm. I had to admit. I wasn't that excited to see him anymore either. After my last encounter with Kenneth it felt wrong to sleep with Malcolm. Being with Kenneth was incredible and it was difficult for me to see anyone else. The man was growing on me.

"Can't you tell him I'm sick or something? I just can't do it."

She laughed. "Oh now you want to back off Malcolm."

"Please don't say I told you so," I said.

She placed her hand on my leg.

"I won't," she said. "No matter how badly I want to."

I dipped my head back down.

"Please tell him to go away."

She slapped my leg.

"Can't do that. You need to pay the bills. You can't quit so you might as well get paid to be here."

She stood from the bed and fixed her dress.

"I have to go mingle," she said waking toward the door. "Oh, Malcolm is in room 208," she said before exiting.

I knew she was correct. If I had to be here, I might as well get paid for it. I had an education fund and I couldn't let my feelings for Kenneth get in the way of it. I lay on the bed for a few minutes before I sat up. I walked over to the mirror by the wet bar and fixed my dress and hair. I took a deep breath and finally left. I walked down the hall to room 208.

The door clicked opened and I entered a dark quiet room. My eyes had to adjust to the lack of light. I took a few steps further into the room. The door shut behind me and I jumped.

"Malcolm?"

I heard nothing as I ventured closer to the bed. Suddenly I was grabbed from behind and a hand clamped across my mouth. Pressed up against the hard body of a man, I was petrified. I tried to scream but his hand over my mouth only muffled the sound.

He was strong and managed to force me onto the bed with his body on top of me. I began to kick and claw at him. It was no use. Finally his hand moved away from my mouth and immediately I began to scream.

"Help! Help!"

"Kim, shut the fuck up!"

I went silent. I knew that voice. He climbed off me and began to laugh.

"Calm the fuck down."

I rolled over and glared at him.

"Malcolm! What is your problem? Why would you do that?"

I could felt tears fill the corners of my eyes.

He continued to laugh.

"Next time don't make me wait."

I panicked. The adrenaline and fear that kicked in was still pumping through my veins. I began to cry.

"Whoa, calm down! Don't do that," he said coming over to the bed. He slid in next to me.

"You scared the shit out of me," I said with tears still streaming down my face. "I thought I was going to end up like Wendy."

Instead of comforting me he began to laugh again.

"Oh shit. I didn't think about that. I only wanted to scare you a little."

I wiped the tears from my face. I was so angry. I tried to climb off the bed but he grabbed me and pulled me over.

"Where are you going?"

He licked his lips then leaned down and placed them on mine. I wanted to pull away but I knew how violent Malcolm could be. I kissed him back and felt his body melt into me.

"You smell so good baby," he said pulling my halter top dress down exposing my breasts. He moved down to take one into his mouth. No matter how angry I was, I couldn't help the way my body responded.

My nipples hardened and I could feel my pussy soaking through my panties. His hand slid up my leg between my thighs until he reached the meeting between them and stroked me there. I moaned and he chuckled.

"You like that?" he asked.

I felt guilty for enjoying himself. My mind went to Kenneth and what he would think of this situation. Did he know Malcolm was my client? Did he care?

Malcolm sat up and began to yank off my panties. Once he got them off, he began to undress.

"Touch yourself," he said pulling his shirt over his head.

I hesitated.

"Touch yourself...now!" he demanded.

I let my hand slide down my body until it reached my soaking wet sex. I caressed my clit.

"Slide your fingers inside. I want to see you fuck yourself."

I obeyed sliding in two fingers. I pulled them in and out while he watched. He climbed on the bed and pulled them out placing them in his mouth. He sucked each finger keeping his eyes on me. Then he pulled back to grab a condom. He unwrapped and put it on.

Then he was on me sliding inside of me. His hand slid up my body to my neck. I knew what was coming. I tensed as he squeezed my neck cutting off my air supply. His pace increased and became more aggressive and hurried. Finally he moved his hand from around my neck. I coughed as air rushed back into my lungs.

"Turn over,' he said pulling out. I turned anticipating him fucking me from behind. He did but with an added twist. I felt a belt wrap around my neck and pull tight. My eyes enlarged and I tried to flip back over.

What was his problem?

"Where are you going? Get that ass back in the air."

He pulled the belt even tighter.

I tried to yell but I couldn't breathe. He didn't have a safe word… not like it would have mattered. He entered me again holding on to the belt and slapping my ass in the process. The harder he slapped the more turned on I became.

I closed my eyes and focused on taking tiny breaths through my nose as he hit my g-spot. To my surprise, I felt my orgasm building. I came hard still fighting for air.

How did he know such aggression and pain would feel so good?

He came shortly after growling and finally releasing the belt. He dropped beside me breathing heavily. I laid there with the belt still around my neck relishing in the amazing orgasm I just had.

Suddenly he climbed off the bed and grabbed his pants. He pulled some money from his pocket and tossed it on me.

"Take it and don't ask any fucking questions."

I grabbed the money and squeezed it in my hands. I pulled my knees up to my chest. I didn't care that I was half naked. I dipped my head down to my knees and wished   I   was   someplace   else.

CHAPTER 21

Malcolm

I wasn't a morning person. Receiving early morning calls from Tony was not something I was willing to get used to. He called and asked me to come down to the lounge for a meeting. Of course when I arrived at *Inferno*, he was nowhere to be found.

I leaned against the bar and waited. I watched as Luciano directed a contractor where to install surveillance cameras. In a place like this, cameras were usually frowned upon. However, between Luciano's insisting and the death of Wendy, cameras were now being installed in the common areas.

They, Tony hoped, would be a deterrent. He also took my advice and hired some more security to secure the halls near the VIP rooms.

"Hey Malcolm," Luciano said coming over to sit down next to me. "Do you think this will work?"

I took a sip of my coffee.

"It might work but it also might scare off a few regulars. You guys really think your clients are going to stand for cameras?"

"Well we have no choice. We have got to do something to protect these women."

I huffed and took another sip of my coffee.

"What do *you* think we should do?" he asked.

"I say the security guards Tony hired should be enough."

"We have to be sure," he replied walking back over to the men in the corner.

Suddenly, I felt a hand glide up my back and across my head. Only one woman touches me that way. I turned and came face to face with Ashley.

"What can I do for you?" I asked.

"Hey daddy," she said. "I'm ready to be tied up and choked until I come all over your dick."

I cringed at her words. If this had been months ago, she would have been fair game. However, once you've had access to filet mignon it's highly unlikely you're going to go back to eating hamburger.

"Ashley, not now. I'm busy."

"Really?" she said. "You don't look busy to me."

"Well, I am."

"You're too busy for this?" she asked.

She was wearing a tank top with a low cut V-neck. Her short skirt showed off her long beautiful legs. It was not an outfit one would wear in the fall, but it was sexy as hell. I must admit, I started to get hard remembering the old times.

"I'll pass," I said.

"Come on Malcolm. You don't have to wait until tonight to taste this."

"What are you doing here this early anyway?" I questioned.

"I came to see Tony," she said. "But since we're both here..." she took a step closer and wrapped her arms around my neck. "I say we make up for lost time and fuck in every room upstairs."

"I say we call this thing off."

The smile on her face faded and she glared at me.

"What does that mean?" she asked.

I grabbed her arms and slid them from around my neck. "There will be no more me seeing you or paying you."

She took a step back and placed her hands on her hips. "What are you saying?"

I sighed.

"Let me make this clear. I am no longer your client. We are no longer fucking."

She raised an eyebrow. "You're kidding right?"

I shook my head.

"Look, I don't know how much clearer I can make it. It's just business. I have a new bitch I'm paying and that doesn't leave much room or money left for you," I informed her.

She looked appalled and in disbelief. Then she began to giggle that turned into a full on belly laugh.

I just stared at her. *She was fucking crazy.*

"What's so funny?" I asked.

"I heard rumors but I didn't know this bullshit was true," she said still chuckling.

All of a sudden her laughter stopped and anger flashed across her face.

"That bitch!" she said.

She stopped for a second then took a deep breath.

"Wendy, God rest her soul, beat her ass and she still hasn't learned her lesson."

"Ashley, I don't know what you are yammering about but I have shit to do." I said walking away from her toward the front entrance. Fuck Tony. I had business at the office I needed to handle.

"So you're just going to fuck the same girl your brother is trying to wife?" I heard her say.

That stopped me in my tracks. I turned to look at her. She had a smug look on her face. I could tell she knew something I didn't.

I approached.

"What are you talking about?"

"Oh you don't know about Kim and Kenneth?" she said. "Kenneth is bringing her flowers and kissing her ass. That's what got that bitch beat up by Wendy."

It took a minute to process the information. Kenneth was bringing Kim flowers? Then it hit me. Kim was the special woman at the lounge Kenneth's been swooning over. My heart began to race and my head ached.

"What's the matter? Is baby brother stealing your new client?' she teased. "Looks like you're fucking your future sister-in-law," she laughed. "If only I could be a fly on the wall at family gatherings…"

"Ashley!" I exclaimed. "Get the fuck away from me before I mess you up."

"Don't take it out on me," she said. "Let's just forget about Kim, go upstairs and pull out the toys."

She approached me again.

"I have a shiny new pair of handcuffs you can use."

I was livid at Kenneth and Kim. Ashley was only fueling my anger. I grabbed her arm and pushed her against the bar knocking stools over in the process. My hand left her arm and went to her neck. I squeezed. Her eyes looked like they were going to pop out of her head.

The anger I felt was…different. I had been upset before but there was a new sensation surrounding it. I knew it had to do with Kim. I've been looking for someone like her for a long time and the thought of my brother or anyone being with her was making me feel things I hadn't felt in a while.

Jealousy?

Heartache?

I had never competed with my brother for a woman and I wasn't going to start now.

"Come near me again, Ashley, and I will fucking kill you. Do you understand?"

I could feel her try to nod.

"Good," I replied.

I let her go. She reached for her neck and bent over gasping for air. I knew next time I saw Kim...I was going to do the same.

I turned around to see Luciano staring at me. I grabbed my cup of coffee off the bar and walked out the front door.

CHAPTER 22

Kenneth

A cool breeze flowed through the open window. She shivered slightly as she grinded on me. My hands glided across her smooth chocolate thighs. I watched her face as she rode me. Her eyes were closed and gently she caressed her breasts. Soft moans escaped from her parted lips. My body wanted to speed up the rhythm aching to feel the ultimate bliss. Yet I didn't want to distract her from the pleasure she was feeling.

Suddenly she increased her pace with her hands on my chest. I took that as a sign to take over. I gripped her hips and bounced her up and down.

"Oh, yes," she moaned.

I could feel her sex tighten around me and I responded by groaning. Her moans increased in volume and I knew she was close.

I was right.

She came digging her nails into my chest. I pulled her against me holding her in a tight embrace as she came. I let the pleasure ripple through her body a moment before I rolled us both over putting myself on top.

She let out a contented sigh as I took a nipple into my mouth. I moved from her breast and sat up. I slid inside of her caressing her legs as I pulled them up onto my shoulders.

I picked up my pace, stroking and placing kisses on her calves and ankles. The only sounds that could be heard was moaning and my thighs slapping against hers.

I came hard with my face pressed against her ankle. I dropped her legs and collapsed on the bed beside her.

"That was amazing," I said staring at the ceiling.

"It was," she agreed.

We laid there savoring the aftermath of our orgasms for a few minutes. I looked over and saw a stack of books on the desk next to me. I turned my head to look at Kim.

"How much does it cost?" I asked.

She rolled onto her side. Her eyes were trained on me.

"How much does what costs?" she frowned at me. "My services?"

I shook my head.

"No," I replied smiling. "Your books and classes."

She raised an eyebrow. "Why do you want to know?"

I could tell she was perplexed by my question but I had my reasons.

"I was wondering." I said rolling over onto my side to face her. "I mean…maybe I could help you out."

She giggled.

"Are you trying to take care of me Kenneth? Do you want to be my sugar daddy?" she asked.

I would have laughed too if I wasn't so serious about the situation.

"Look, I just don't want you working at *Inferno* anymore."

I watched her hand move. She traced the scar on my head with her finger. "You're cute when you're worried."

"Kim, I'm serious."

She sighed.

"I don't want to work there anymore either. But it's not like I have a choice."

I reached out and caressed her cheek. She was beautiful but she had more than her beauty going for her. I hated she felt she had no options.

"It's your life. You have a choice. I know your education is important to you, but there are other things you can do. Don't let April and Sasha tell you otherwise."

Her brow furrowed and she shook her head.

"No, it has nothing to do with April, Sasha or my education. It's Tony."

It was my turn to be confused.

"What does Tony have to do with it?"

She sat up and scooted her body until her back was against the head board and her knees were in her chest.

"Tony called me. He told me if I tried to leave his employment, he would make my life miserable."

"Tony only says those things to scare you or intimidate you into staying." I informed her. "Let me talk to him. He's harmless."

I knew Tony did whatever he could to keep girls around. Calling them and threatening them was one of his tactics.

Her eyes went wide.

"Harmless? Kenneth you can't talk to him. It might make things worse," she began. "April told me he doesn't let anyone leave. She said Abigail wanted to leave…and she ended up dead. Maybe Sarah and Wendy wanted to leave too. I'm not trying to end up like them."

Her words caught me off guard.

"What are you saying? Tony killed Abigail, Wendy and Sarah?"

She nodded.

I stared at her to make sure she was serious. When I was convinced she believed every word, I broke out into laughter. She grabbed a pillow and slapped me with it.

"It's not funny Kenneth."

I laughed harder. So that was the rumor going around the lounge? When I was finally able to regain my composure, I sat up next to her on the bed. I grabbed her hand.

"Abigail, sadly, killed herself and Sarah." I informed her.

"What...really?" she asked.

I nodded.

She sat for a minute with her mouth opened trying to absorb the information. Then she looked over at me.

"What about Wendy?" she asked. "Who killed her?"

I didn't want to talk about Wendy...

"Kim, Tony may come off as ruthless but he's a big Teddy Bear. He's not capable of that kind of violence."

"Are you sure?" she asked.

I could tell this really bothered her. She was chewing on a fingernail gazing off into the distance.

"Kim!" I called.

She turned to stare at me. I placed my lips on hers and enveloped her in a kiss. I pulled back and looked her in the eye.

"You don't have to be afraid. I won't let anyone hurt you."

She began to search my eyes with hers. "You really mean that don't you?"

I nodded.

"Do you want to quit?" I asked her.

She nodded. I could see tears forming in her eyes.

"Then quit." I said pulling her against me.

A cold breeze blew from the window through the room. I pulled the covers up over our naked bodies. She cuddled against me and we fell asleep in each others' arms.

CHAPTER 23

Kimberly

"Mopey is not a good look on you," April said sitting down next to me.

I was hiding out in my little corner of the lounge pouting and wishing I didn't have to be here. I crossed my legs and folded my arms across my chest.

"Well, that's the look you guys are going to get."

She shook her head.

"I don't understand you," she said. "You got what you wanted. Malcolm Johnson is a great client. He is sexy and for years he paid Ashley well and not once did he ask for her exclusively."

She punched me in the arm. "Girl, you got the holy grail."

I didn't feel that way. I felt like I was trapped in an emotional dilemma. I hadn't told anyone about my budding relationship with Kenneth. I'm not stupid. I figured out quickly Kenneth didn't know Malcolm slept with women at the lounge. He held his brother in the highest regards and believed he was faithful to his wife despite the many hours Malcolm spent at *Inferno*. How would he feel when he found out Malcolm and I slept together? I didn't want to be the one to tell him.

I arrived at the club today on a mission. Tony refused to let me quit so I came up with a plan. My goal was to wait for Malcolm to arrive and hope I could reason with him.

"I'm only here to ask Malcolm to request someone else," I replied.

"You really think that's going to happen?"

"Maybe if I tell him I don't want him, he won't want me."

She frowned.

"Since when do you not want him?"

I didn't want to confess to April that I hadn't wanted Malcolm since Kenneth swept me off my feet. What I really wanted was the other Johnson brother.

"Since I realized I didn't want to work here anymore," I replied. "Malcolm is the only one who wants me. Maybe if he withdraws his request, Tony won't have a problem with me quitting."

She chuckled.

"Tony will always have a problem with you quitting. I don't see why you can't just enjoy what you have with Malcolm."

Because it would jeopardize what I have with Kenneth. I wanted to tell her but I held my tongue.

"Here you are?" I heard.

April and I looked up to find Sasha standing in front of us.

"Are you going to mope over here in this corner forever?" she asked.

April laughed. "That's what I'm saying."

I heaved a sigh. "Look, I'm not going to be happy until I leave this place."

I felt tears in my eyes. I hadn't realized this issue had me so emotional. Sasha sat on the other side of me and began to rub my back.

"I hate seeing you like this," April said leaning in and wrapping her arms around me. I laid my head on her shoulder.

"Are we having a party over here?"

We all looked up to see Ashley.

"We were kinda trying to have a moment." April said.

I let go of April and jumped to my feet. I didn't want Ashley standing over me. The mere presence of her spelled trouble.

"Oh Kim, you look so hot in that dress," Ashley said.

I swallowed the lump in my throat.

"Aren't you going to say thank you?"

"Ashley, don't you have a client?" April asked.

"Well, normally I do. It is Thursday. However," she said placing her hand on her hip. "This used to be Malcolm's night. Apparently he has other plans now."

I knew where this was going. She took a step toward me.

April and Sasha stood.

"Ashley," April began.

Ashley held up a hand.

"I just want to congratulate Kim on being a sneaky bitch that has no shame in stealing clients."

"I don't have time for this," I responded.

I was frustrated and upset. The last thing I needed was Ashley in my face.

"Bitch please. You think you're dismissing me. I'll fuck you up like Wendy did."

At the mention of my fight with Wendy, I was on edge.

She took another step forward and was so close to me our noses almost touched. I moved backward.

"Back off Ashley!" I exclaimed.

She moved closing the gap between us.

"Ashley if you don't back up…"

"What! If I don't back up what are you going to do about it?"

"Kim," April said. "Let's go."

I turned to reach for my purse off the couch. Ashley grabbed my arm to swing me around. I had enough of people putting their hands on me. No way was I going to get attacked first this time. I swung and hit her hard on the side of her face. She stumbled and fell backwards in her heels. Before she could hit the ground however, she reached out and grabbed a handful of my braids. The pain was excruciating and I relented falling to the ground with her. I had a feeling she pulled my hair from my head. Now I was really angry. She fell on her back and I crawled on top of her. I began to pound her in the face.

All the frustration, pain and anger I felt, I took out on her. She put up her hands but I didn't stop. I saw an empty glass on a nearby table. I reached for it and would have smashed it in her face…if someone hadn't grabbed my arm.

I looked up to see Sasha's eyes wide as she pulled the glass from my hand. She wrapped her arms around my waist and pulled me off Ashley. I was still in fight mode kicking and screaming.

"Whoa, calm down!" Sasha said.

"Let me go!" I yelled.

"Not until you calm down!"

I watched as Luciano helped Ashley to her feet. I began to realize how crazy I was being. Her nose was bleeding and my head and hand hurt like hell.

I began to calm down taking deep breaths. Sasha could tell I was done. She let me go. I walked over to the leather couch and grabbed my purse. I walked past the stunned and silent crowd toward the front door. I was stopped however before I had a chance to leave.

Standing in my way was Tony.

Apparently he came out of his office when he was told about the fight. Explains why the crowd was quiet.

"Kim," he said with a look of disdain on his face. The frown set deeply into his features.

I was shocked he remembered my name. That may not be a good thing.

"Don't you have an appointment with Malcolm tonight?" he asked calmly. He was so composed it terrified me.

"Yes," I replied.

"Then go upstairs and clean up."

"I'm leaving," I announced looking him in the eye.

He came toward me. He grabbed my arm and yanked me against him.

"You aren't going anywhere," he said through clinched teeth.

My breath caught in my throat. His eyes were narrowed and his brow was furrowed. I was petrified

"Now go upstairs, clean up and wait for Malcolm."

I didn't want to but I was too afraid not to. He released me and I reluctantly followed his command.

CHAPTER 24

I grabbed the plastic bag filled with ice and brought it over to the bed where she was sitting. I dropped down to my knees in front of her.

"Let me see that hand," I said.

She held it out to me. Despite her dark skin, her fist was reddened and beginning to swell. I placed the small bag of ice on her it and held it there. She didn't say much. She just stared at the wall. I could tell she was fighting back tears.

"Do you want to talk about it?" I asked.

I wanted to make her feel comfortable enough to confide in me.

Kim turned to look at me. A tear cascaded down her cheek and she wiped it away with her free hand.

"I just wish I'd never started working here. I don't belong here." She reached out and put her hand on my shoulder. "You know you can help me, right? You can talk to Tony and get him to let me go."

I shook my head.

"I'm not sure who told you that, but I can't do a damn thing about Tony."

She sighed.

"April told me I was wasting my time." Another tear fell but this time she didn't do anything about it. "I just want to leave here and never look back."

I could see the pain in her eyes. She was sad and vulnerable. Right now…she was just my type.

She looked toward the door.

"I hope Tony doesn't come up here."

"Nah," I said. "He's not coming now that I'm here."

I continued to hold the ice on her hand. My eyes began to wander all over her body. I yearned to taste her again. She turned me on with her pouty lips and thick thighs. I loved her long braids and the almond shape of her eyes. I almost got hard by just looking at her. But only one thing would get me off…

Kim was going to be so good. I hadn't thought about what it would be like to come while the life drained from her face. She meant so much to me that it hadn't crossed my mind. But now that I had her here…I knew it would be incredible.

"Is it painful?" I asked.

She nodded.

"My hand hurts but my head feels worse. I think she may have pulled out my hair," she replied.

"Well, I have just the right thing to make you feel better and ease the pain a little." I told her.

I grabbed her hand and put it on top of the bag of ice. I stood and walked to the side of the room that held a few glasses near a sink and a refrigerator. There was no wet bar in this room. However, there was a pre-stocked fridge. There were a few bottles of wine, beer, some champagne and a couple bottles of vodka. The wine would have to do. It was a dry red and hopefully would mask the taste of the drugs.

I grabbed a glass from the side of the sink and poured her some. With my back to her, I pulled a small bottle from the inside pocket of my suit jacket. It contained a mixture of crushed up Xanax and sleeping pills. *I was always prepared for another opportunity.* I dumped some of the medication into the glass of wine. I didn't put in enough to kill her. Just enough to knock her out. I wanted to handle the rest with my bare hands. I didn't see a spoon so I stirred the drugs with my finger. When I was satisfied, I turned and walked the drink over to her.

"Here you go. A nice glass of wine."

"Thank you," she said.

I grabbed the bag of ice and sat it on the floor then handed her the wine. I sat back down next to her.

I watched as she took a big gulp. Then she handed the glass to me.

It wasn't empty.

"Here," I said handing it back to her. "You'll feel better if you drink it all."

She shrugged, took the glass from me and downed the rest. She sat the glass on the carpeted floor and sighed.

I placed my hand on her back and began to caress it. I fought the urge to wrap my fingers around her neck. I needed the drugs to kick in before that could happen. I could see her hands go to her eyes as they began to droop. The meds were beginning to affect her and soon my time would come.

I leaned in and kissed her on the neck. She moaned in reply. That fueled my desire and I placed more kisses. My hand trailed up her bare legs anticipating reaching the meeting between them. I moved her hand and placed it on my now hardened member. My breathing was labored and my heart felt like it was going to beat out of my chest.

I bowed to kiss her on the neck again, but was stopped when the door swung open. In walked a determined April. I Immediately put some distance between Kim and me. April stood there with her hands on her hips. I silently kicked myself for not locking the door.

"God, Kim. I've been looking all over this shithole for you. Are you okay?"she asked rushing over to us.

She sat on the other side of her. She reached up and touched a spot on Kim's head.

"Girl, she ripped out a couple of your braids!"

Kim began to giggle.

"I know," she said falling backwards on the bed still laughing. I looked at her face and knew she was high. I would have been able to take advantage of that if it hadn't been for April. I felt frustrated and was fuming at the intrusion.

April looked dismayed. Her eyes darted over to me. I shrugged my shoulders. I hoped April wouldn't suspect I had anything to do with Kim's weird behavior.

"Kim, are you okay?" she asked.

"I'm fine…" she said slurring her words. "I don't feel any pain."

April again looked over at me. She folded her arms across her chest. "What the hell is wrong with her? Did she take something?"

My anger was consuming me inside and barely allowed me to speak. April was standing in my way of vital release. I needed this more than I needed air. Yet, I knew I was going to have to come up with something. I reached down and grabbed the glass from the floor.

"She just had several glasses of wine," I lied.

April narrowed her eyes while glaring at Kim.

"Kim, you're a fucking light weight," she responded shaking her head.

She reached over and pulled her up by her arm. Kim's head drooped and her body swayed from side to side.

April sighed and looked at me.

"Can you help me get her out of here and to my car? I need to get her home. She is no good to anyone like this."

I didn't agree. I had an opportunity to pursue the ultimate release but was stopped by an overzealous friend. I didn't say a word, however, as I stood and helped Kim up. I put her arm around my neck and let her lean on me.

"I'm going to get you out of here, okay Kim?" April said as we walked toward the door. "Fuck Tony!"

Kim giggled.

"Fuck Tony," she mimicked.

I was determined this wasn't going to be my last chance with Kim. She was more precious to me than any of the other women. That would make extinguishing her life much more satisfying. She would be my ultimate goal. I knew killing her would be glorious and next time, April wouldn't be around to stand in my way.

CHAPTER 25

Kenneth

I walked across the polished tile floor hearing my shoes click with each step. I was at *Inferno* in the early morning hours when the lounge was empty and the girls were all gone preparing for the night.

I was here to see Tony.

I had a few choice words for him and I didn't plan to leave until I was heard loud and clear. After her fight with Ashley, Kim was determined not to work at the lounge anymore. And as if on cue, Tony began his campaign of calling Kim and making threats. She was terrified. I was furious. I promised her I would handle it and today that was what I intended to do.

I reached the office door and went inside without knocking. Once I entered, all talking ceased. Eyes were on me. Tony seemed happy until he saw it was me at the door. The smile faded from his face. I could tell he was expecting someone else.

"You're not Malcolm," he said. "Did he send his little brother in his place?"

"I'm not here on behalf of Malcolm," I replied.

I looked around the room and realized they had a full house. Luciano was present as well as Tony's two bodyguards and two security guards. Mario Santino, Tony's cousin, was there and three other men I had never seen before.

"Okay," Tony said. "Then why are you here?"

"I'm here to talk to you…" I looked around at the group. "in private."

"Well then, you have to wait. As you can see we have an important meeting going on," he said. "All we're waiting for is Malcolm."

"I need to speak to you now." I demanded.

He looked at me and frowned. "Can it wait?"

"No," I replied. "it can't wait."

He leaned back in his leather chair and folded his arms across his chest.

"Well, tell it. Whatever you need to say you can say it in front of everyone here."

I took a step forward and approached his desk.

"I'm here about Kim."

He raised an eyebrow.

"Kim?" he asked. "Who's Kim?"

Luciano spoke up. "You know, the dark skin girl with the long braids. She and Ashley fought the other day."

He nodded. "Ahhh, Kim."

He looked at me unimpressed. "You interrupted my meeting over some bitch?"

His words infuriated me. I took a deep breath and let it out before I spoke. "She's not just some bitch."

"Why are you here about her and why couldn't this wait?" he asked.

"Kim has received a series of calls from you threatening bodily harm if she doesn't return to work. I'm here to tell you she isn't coming back. Stop threatening her."

He sighed.

"I'm sorry you came all this way for something that's not going to happen. If she's getting a call from me then she needs to get her ass back to work."

I took another step toward him.

"I'm sorry you feel the need to waste your time. She's not coming back here."

He sat up and leaned forward against his desk. He narrowed his eyes at me.

"Tell me, Kid," he said. "Why are you so concerned about this girl?"

I rolled my eyes. I hated being called kid. I was a grown ass man! Being Malcolm's younger brother, however, made Tony give me that title.

"She's my client. She doesn't want to work here anymore. Threatening her is wrong and it should stop."

"She's your client huh?"

I nodded.

"Let me rephrase my question. Since when have you ever took on any of these ladies as a client and cared about what I do with my employees?" Tony questioned.

He cocked his head to the side. Then he smiled.

"Oh I get it," he chuckled. "Malcolm told me about you."

I had no clue what he was talking about. I folded my arms across my chest. I was irritated.

"Malcolm said you like to save ho's," he said.

The room broke out into laughter.

"You're smitten with this girl, aren't you?" Tony asked.

I didn't respond to his question.

"No more threats Tony." I pointed my finger at him. "You're going to let her quit."

He stopped laughing and his smiled disappeared. He looked around the room and then back at me. The men in the room went silent.

"I don't have to do anything," he said standing. "She has a VIP client who wants her exclusively. She better come back or I'm going to make sure she wished she were dead."

His sudden outpour of anger didn't scare me. He always wanted to come across as frightening or intimidating. Especially now, in this room, he wanted to throw his weight around. I wasn't afraid of him.

"You come near her and you're going to wish you never fucked with me." I said approaching his desk.

I wanted to ring his neck.

His largest body guard, Sugar, stepped forward. I'm sure his goal was to fuck me up or throw me out. Tony stopped him.

"Kenneth," he said sitting back down in his chair. "I don't appreciate being threatened."

"Doesn't feel good, does it?" I replied.

He glared at me. Then he began to laugh again. I didn't find anything funny.

"Kid," he chuckled. "Calm down. We can't let some bitch come between us. I like you. I really do. However, Kim stays."

"I don't think you understand. Kim is done here. End of story."

He shook his head with a smile on his face.

"How about this. I'll let her go when her VIP doesn't want her anymore."

That was good enough for me. I just needed to know who this VIP was. Then I could beat the shit out of him and make him leave her alone.

"Who is her VIP?" I asked.

He chuckled and shook his head.

"Ask your brother."

I didn't know what Malcolm had to do with this.

"Why can't you just tell me?"

"Look, Kenneth, we're busy now. That's all the time I have for this bullshit. Talk to your brother."

I had no clue why Tony didn't just tell me who the hell this guy was.

"Why am I asking Malcolm?"

Tony sighed.

Luciano spoke up. "Ken, just ask Malcolm."

I wasn't completely happy with my conversation with Tony. I left his office still upset yet even more determined to free Kim from this place.

They wanted me to talk to Malcolm so that was what I was going to do. I knew there was a chance my brother wouldn't help me. He'd be a hard sell seeing as he didn't want me messing around with the girls at the lounge.

However, he didn't understand how Kim made me feel. She was the one and I just had to convince my brother of that. If I appealed to him, hopefully he would help me.

He had to.

CHAPTER 26

Malcolm

This is bullshit! I thought as I approached *Inferno*. I was irritable and cranky. It had been a while since I've had sex and I didn't like this feeling. Kim had been a no-show to several appointments and I was getting pissed.

I had Tony call and threaten her. I needed her back to work... The kind of sex I wanted was a no go with my wife. The last time I tried to choke her she threatened to call the police. Since then, I've been fulfilling my fantasies at the club.

My brother was to blame for my predicament. He was on another crusade to save to a ho'. I attended a meeting this morning with Tony and according to him, my brother showed up flexing and demanding he let Kim quit. I wasn't having that.

I had to do something. I decided I would have a little talk with Kim. My brother was too stubborn to listen, but I knew Kim could be persuaded. I just needed to get to her.

I walked into the lounge and approached the bar. I took a seat and searched for Sasha. I found her at the other end talking with a patron. I waved her over to me.

She approached placing her hand on her hip.

"What can I get you, Malcolm? The usual?"

I shook my head.

"No," I said. "I'm looking for Kim."

She pursed her lips together before she spoke.

"Kim isn't here. She hasn't come back since her fight with Ashley."

"I know she isn't here." I said.

Sasha looked perplexed. "Then why are you..." realization dawned on her face and her eyes widened. She shook her head. "No way, Malcolm."

"Come on, Sasha. I just need to see her."

"No," she said. "I'm not giving you her address."

"Sasha, I'm not just some regular client. She needs to see me as much as I need to see her."

"She doesn't need you Malcolm and you know that."

I wasn't going to get what I needed from Sasha. My only hope was to talk Luciano into giving it to me. Tony has a rule that clients cannot have a girl's address. It was for the girls' safety. Even when I asked him, he wouldn't give me Kim's address.

"Where is Luc?" I asked looking around the room.

She heaved a sigh and rolled her eyes. "He's not here and don't ask him."

This was a blank mission. This trip was a waste of time. I couldn't get to Kim tonight and the last thing I wanted to do was go home. So, in the meantime, I'm just going to get shit-faced.

"Well, then give me a shot of whiskey." I told Sasha.

She poured me a shot and slid it over to me. I downed it, tapped my glass and slid it back over to her. She laughed and poured me another. I quickly devoured that one as well.

"Slow down," she warned.

I ignored her advice and indicated I wanted one more. She slid another over to me. I picked it up and attempted to drink it when I felt a hand slide up my back. I looked over to find Ashley taking the stool next to me.

"Hey sexy," she said.

She reached over, grabbed my shot from my hand and drank it. I watched her closely as she slammed the glass down on the counter.

She was acting suspicious. Especially since the last time I saw her I told her I would fuck her up. I noticed a scratch on her face. I assumed it came from her fight with Kim.

"Nice scar," I said motioning for another drink.

"Yes it is. It gives me another reason to kill that bitch Kim," she said through a forced smile.

"Really? Because I kind of like it."

She smiled leaning in closer and lowering her voice. "Oh you do? Why is that?"

I turned my stool to completely face her. I lowered my voice.

"Gives me something else to look at while your lips are wrapped around my dick."

I could feel the alcohol flowing through my veins and I felt warm all over. Sasha passed me another shot and I drank that as well.

Ashley laughed. "I thought you were done with me."

If Kim were here, there wouldn't be a need for her. As it was, I was hard up and needed to get laid.

"I don't see Kim around, do you?" I replied. "You can keep talking about her or we can go upstairs and fuck like we used to."

She licked her lips. "Well then, let's go."

She led me by the hand upstairs to my favorite room. When we entered I didn't hesitate. I slammed the door shut, locked it and began to undo the buckle on my pants.

"I want you on the bed on your knees," I demanded letting my pants and underwear fall to my ankles.

"What?" No foreplay?" she asked.

I stopped and looked behind me. I turned and looked back at her.

"Are you talking to me?" I asked.

She laughed. Walking over to the bed, she slowly began to undress. I pulled off my pants and underwear. I tossed them on the nearby couch. When she was naked, she laid on the bed and spread her legs wide.

"I said on your knees. I want that ass in the air."

She shook her head. "I think you want to eat me out first."

I frowned at her. Then I laughed. "You have to be fucking kidding me. The entire time we had sex I've never once gone down on you. I wouldn't put my lips down there for all the money in the world."

She looked upset and put off by my statement. Too bad. It was the truth.

She climbed off the bed and began to redress.

"What the fuck are you doing?"

"You can't eat me out but I bet you go down on Kim."

The bitterness in her voice was unmistakable.

"Look, I'm losing my erection. Are we going to fuck or what?"

She gave me a dirty look. I've seen that expression before. It's the one my wife's been giving me lately. Her eyes were low and her nose was clenched like something smelled bad.

"Noooo...you don't want to fuck me. You want to fuck Kim," she began to rant. "That's fine. Fuck Kim. I don't need your raggedy dick anyway. I can get any man or woman here I want."

Fine with me, I thought. She was just a fuck of desperation. I shook my head and began to put my underwear and pants back on.

She sat back on the bed and crossed her legs.

"Oh, we're not done, Malcolm," she said shaking her foot by the ankle.

"Oh yes we are," I said snapping my belt into place.

"What about my money?"

Money? We didn't even do anything.

"What money?"

"Just because you are sleeping with Kim doesn't mean you don't owe me. You still have a tab with me."

I laughed.

"I don't owe you a damn thing."

"You have an obligation to me. If you don't pay, I'll make sure your little wifey knows all about your years of escapades at this lounge."

I glared at her. She knew she was never to mention my wife or my kids. Now she was threatening to...

"What are you saying Ashley. Are you trying to blackmail me?"

I took a few steps toward her. She stood and moved from the bed and away from me.

"Of course I'm blackmailing you," she replied. "And I can do it to. I've already met your wife."

Her words brought tightness to my chest.

"What are you talking about?"

"I met Evelyn. I found your address and followed her and your kids to the park. We talked. Her kids played with my kids. She is such a nice lady. If you want to keep her you'll pay me my money."

After hearing her words, I wasn't able to understand or explain what came over me. The anger burned so hot and intense. I'd never experienced such an emotion before. It's like I blacked out and when I came to I had her on the floor choking the shit out of her. She was kicking, scratching and trying to scream.

I continued to compress her windpipe. It felt oddly good to see her eyes bulge out and plead for release.

"What did you say to my wife?!" I screamed.

She pulled at my hands and arms trying to get me to stop. Her attempts at freedom eventually became weaker. I let go.

She rolled over holding her throat, hacking up a lung. The last thing I needed was for her to tell my wife anything. The only way to keep her quiet was to teach her a lesson. She sat up and looked at me. She knew how close she came. She climbed to her feet, stumbled toward the door, unlocked it and ran out of the room.

I wasn't done with her. She needed to learn not to fuck with me and my family.

CHAPTER 27

I watched her stumble down the stairs. The look on her face spelled out fear. Her eyes were wide and her makeup was a smeared mess on her face. Her clothes were disheveled and her hair was not in the neat bun it was in before.

Her appearance garnered the attention momentarily from a few patrons. It must be why she headed toward the back offices instead of the main lounge area. I excused myself from the group of gentleman I was talking to and casually followed her. I stayed a good distance behind. I saw her twist and turn through the back halls stumbling in her heels. She headed in the direction of the back door.

The back door was heavily secured. Once you exit, you can only return through that door with a key. I watched her push the heavy door open and exit. I waited until the door slammed shut before I followed her out.

When I stepped outside, I expected to see her right away. I didn't. It was dark and there was little light in the alley. Finally I could hear her crying. I let the door close before I followed the sounds. I let her cries lead me a few feet down the alley and around the huge green dumpster. That's where I found her huddled against the brick wall with tears pouring out her eyes and down her cheeks.

When she saw me, she jumped.

"Please…" she said holding up her hand.

"Calm down Ashley. I'm not here to hurt you."

She began to sob, but I could still make out what she wanted to say.

"How am I supposed to believe you? All the men you have in this club just hurt women. We're just sex toys for them to play with."

I crouched down in front of her.

"I'm not sure what you expected working here," I replied.

I knew the women in this club felt men should act like gentlemen. I told them they should find another job if that is what they were expecting.

She sniffed a little then sighed.

"You would think men here would at least see us as human beings. I can't do this anymore."

She was right. The men in this club treated women like blow up dolls. Not to say I'm not one of them. I just happened to be pretty good at pretending I was better than the rest.

She continued to sob and I reached over and placed my hand on her knee.

"Let's go back inside." I said. "You have clients waiting for you."

"No," she responded. "I'm not going back in there."

She stood and attempted to fix her hair and dress.

"I'm just going to go home," she said and promptly began to cry again. "I'm done with this place!"

Then she fell against me and sobbed into my shirt.

I felt uneasy. I didn't come back here to be her shoulder to cry on. She had become a threat to the lounge. I overheard her talking to some girls about information she had on clients and planning to blackmail them. I didn't need that. I had to do what I could to protect *Inferno*.

I pushed her body back and she looked up at me. I could see in her eyes that she wanted me. She licked her lips and I found myself harden a little. Not enough to fuck a woman but enough to know that arousal was on the horizon.

She leaned in for a kiss. I didn't respond the way she wanted me to. I pushed her off me.

"What the fuck are you doing?" she demanded to know.

"Not in a million years Ashley!" This bitch had been with almost every man and woman that walked through the door of the lounge. I wouldn't kiss or fuck her even if my life depended on it.

"Really?" she began to rant. "These new young girls show up and I am useless now. I am old news. I will not be pushed aside. I have bills to pay and kids to feed. If these men don't want me they will pay me no matter what. Even if I have to tell all of their wives what terrible despicable people they are!"

I could feel my body heat up at her words and my head felt like it was going to explode. My anger was growing and I knew one of us wasn't leaving this alley alive.

I took a step toward her and was surprised to see she didn't move. Her anger gave her a bravado I hadn't seen in most of the girls. Most women in the lounge could tell when I was angry. They shriveled at my presence. Not Ashley. Not tonight.

I reached up and placed my hand around her neck. She was so shocked she didn't try to stop me. I pushed her backward until I held her against the brick wall. I continued to squeeze. My hand tightened until her eyes enlarged and I could tell she realized this was life or death.

That is when Ashley began to fight.

She kicked and hit me in groin. I cried out and fell to my knees. Pain radiated throughout my body.

I heard her banging on the locked back door. I looked up to see she had given up on that task and began to stagger down the alley toward the front of the building.

I had to end this now.

I pulled myself together and began to follow her. Once she noticed I was right behind, she began to run. I chased her. When she fell in her heels, I was there to drag her back into the darkness.

"Help!" she screamed.

I needed to shut her up. I straddled her body and with all my might I smashed my fist against her face. I hit her again. The third blow was enough to render her unconscious. It was at that point I could have just choked her until she was gone. But I needed something more. I wanted to make sure she would be dead.

I reached into my pocket and pulled out my switch blade. I normally keep it for protection but tonight I was going to use...to save the lounge.

I took the knife and plunged it deep into her chest. I pulled it out and sunk it in again. I stared at the blood and to my surprise my arousal began to rise. I stabbed her repeatedly. More than what I needed to kill her.

In and out.

Over and over again.

With each penetration of the knife, I felt a relief and a bliss I had never felt before. One last stab to the throat and blood gushed out all over my pants and all over the dark pavement. I stopped stabbing and tried to catch my breath. I climbed off her and just stared at the bloody mess I made.

I unbuttoned my collared shirt and used it to wipe up some of the blood from my arms, hands and face. I needed to get away. I headed down the alley with the knife securely in my pocket. I had a condo not too far from the club. It was an investment I was glad I made. The maze of alleyways would lead me to my place without being seen. My plan was to clean up and head back to the club. I was going to need a drink after this.

CHAPTER 28

Malcolm

My knuckles hit the door.

Blam! Blam! Blam!

It was the third time I knocked. Still no one came to the door. Luciano insisted this was where she and April lived. I saw a car in the driveway and knew someone was home.

I knocked again.

Suddenly the door swung opened. There she stood. Her eyes were squinted and her braids hung loosely down her back and shoulders. She wore a tank top and a pair of shorts that stopped at her shapely thighs.

It appeared she had just woken up.

I looked at my watch. 6:13pm. I looked back up at her.

"Malcolm?" she asked rubbing her eyes with her fingers.

"In the flesh," I replied.

"What are you doing here?"

"I'm here to talk to you," I said pushing past her into the house.

Immediately my eyes were assaulted by the colors and the furniture. *Who decorated this hot mess?* I turned when I heard the door close and lock. Kim stood with her hands on her hips glaring at me.

"What do you really want?" she asked. "I doubt that you came all this way to talk."

I reluctantly walked over and took a seat on a God-awful gold colored couch. I patted the spot next to me. "Come sit down."

She didn't move.

"Look, I honestly came here to talk to you."

"Just talk?" she asked.

I nodded and again patted the spot next to me. Still she hesitated. "Come on…let's have a chat."

Finally she walked over and sat next to me on the sofa. I placed my arm behind her.

"Let me tell you a story," I began.

She sighed and turned to look at me. "Go on…"

"Well, it's a story about Sarah," I said. "I'm not sure if you ever met Sarah before her untimely demise but you are a lot like her."

Kim folded her arms across her chest.

I continued.

"Sarah started at *Inferno* just like you. She was young, sexy, spunky and full of life. She didn't take shit from Ashley or Wendy.

At the mention of Wendy, she squirmed in her seat and instead of folding her arms across her chest, she began to wring her hands.

I didn't blame her. The death of Wendy made everyone uneasy.

"Why are you telling me this?" she questioned.

"Just listen," I said. "Anyway, she was such a hot commodity. Tony had to see what the fuss was all about. So, he requested her."

She raised an eyebrow and her eyes widened.

"No," I laughed. "Tony didn't request you."

She breathed a sigh of relief.

"So, Tony requested her and once he had her, he decided he didn't want anyone else to be with her. That is what started the process of men being able to request women and keep them all to themselves."

I moved my arm from behind her head and placed it on her knee.

"Yet, Tony went further than that. He made her his mistress."

Her brow furrowed and she again folded her arms across her chest.

"He set her up in an apartment, paid her bills and took care of all her needs…as long as she took care of his."

"Are you asking me to be your mistress?" she questioned with her eyes narrowed.

I smiled.

"I'm giving you the opportunity to be my mistress," I corrected. "You no longer have to be an escort. You would be mine with all the benefits."

I didn't see how she could turn me down.

She moved my hand from her knee and stood.

"I'm going to have to pass on this opportunity."

I stood as well.

"I'm offering you a deal of a lifetime. You won't have to worry about anything financially."

"I'm not interested, Malcolm."

I couldn't believe it. Yet deep down I knew why she was turning me down. I just had to hear it from her.

"What could possibly stop you from accepting my offer?"

She looked away unable to meet my eyes. Finally she spoke.

"I just can't do this anymore. I'm moving on from that part of my life."

"It's my brother, isn't it? You and Kenneth have something going on don't you?"

She didn't look surprised I knew. She nodded at my question. I approached her.

There was no longer any amusement in my voice.

"Well that shit ends today. Do you understand me?" I said pointing a finger in her direction. "You and my brother are done."

"You can't tell us what to do," she maintained.

"Oh yes I can. When it comes to my brother I can." I moved in closer. "I am warning you. Stay the fuck away from him."

"Or what?" she asked. "You're going to make my life miserable? Well, you're too late. Someone already beat you to that threat."

I took another step closer. She took a couple of steps backward.

"If you don't stay away from my brother…"

I advanced toward her and she moved until her back was against the front door. I used that position to my advantage.

"I'll make sure he knows about us."

I moved until my body was against hers.

"I'll let him know how hard I make you come."

I ran my hand up her legs until they reached the meeting between her thighs. She sucked in a breath as I stroked her there. Then she pushed me.

'Kenneth knows what I do…what I did for a living. He doesn't care. He'll still want to be with me."

I smiled.

"You're probably right. Unless, he can't live with the fact you've been fucking his own brother. Letting him taste you and you tasting him…"

I could tell she agreed with me. Her eyes were no longer able to meet mine.

"He'll think about that and then he'll move on to the next escort or stripper like he's always done."

Just then my phone rang. I pulled it from my pocket. I saw that it was Tony. I ignored the call. I brought my focus back to Kim. She used my distraction to move away from the wall and stand by the couch.

"What do you mean he will move on to the next stripper or escort?" she asked.

Her eyebrows were furrowed and she began to wring her hands again.

"You don't know my brother the way I do. He does this all the time. He meets a stripper or an escort and starts to pay her bills. He becomes possessive and eventually he only lets her be with him. No family or friends allowed."

She shook her head.

"That doesn't sound like Kenneth."

"Really? How well do you know him? Ask yourself that question. I've had to help him out on numerous occasions. He's stalked women after they've gotten tired of his aggression and possessiveness."

She opened her mouth to speak then closed it.

"I hope you aren't turning me down because he's offering to love you and take care of you. I bet he's even told you 'I won't let anyone hurt you.'"

Her eyes widened at my words.

"You're not an exception to the rule. There will be other women. You'll just be another memory."

She was angry now. I must've hit a nerve. She walked past me and opened the front door.

"I need you to go," she said.

I walked toward the door and stopped right at the threshold.

"Just seriously, think about my offer."

"GET OUT!" she ordered.

My phone began to ring.

I stepped outside and heard the door slam behind me. I knew I had pissed her off but I had a feeling she would come around. It's always easiest to blame the messenger. However, I proposed an offer she couldn't refuse.

The ringing in my pocket started up again. I pulled it out and realized this time it was Luciano.

First Tony, now Luc?

I took a deep breath and let it out. This couldn't be good. I answered the phone.

"Luc, what's going on?" I asked.

Breathing heavily, he spoke.

"Malcolm, we've been trying to get a hold of you."

"I was busy. So what do you need?"

"Another dead body was found."

I felt a knot form in my chest. I closed my eyes.

"Malcolm?"

"Yeah, I'm here. Who died?" I asked.

He sighed.

"It's Ashley," he responded. "She was murdered."

I wasn't surprised.

CHAPTER 29

Kimberly

I sped through red lights and stop signs on my way to the lounge. I vowed I would never step foot in that place again. Luciano called. He said it was April and I didn't let him finish. Still in my pajamas, I jumped in my car and raced toward *Inferno*.

With everything happening at the lounge, I worried about April being there every night. My greatest fear lately was that she would be requested by the wrong client and end up like Wendy. It was why I pleaded with her to follow me out the door. I tried to get her to leave and never look back but she refused. I drove to the lounge hoping my greatest fear wasn't realized.

So many thoughts raced through my head. *What would I do when I arrived? If April was dead, how would I handle that?*

When I got there, my heart sank into my chest. There were flashing red and blue lights everywhere. Tons of people stood outside the lounge filling the parking lot. I parked and headed to the front of the crowd. As much as I dreaded what I was about to learn, I knew I needed to know.

I made my way through the group of bystanders and clients.

"Kim!" I heard someone call.

I looked over and found Sasha squeezing through some of the women. When she reached me, she pulled me into a hug. I moved back and searched her face for answers. The look of sadness and fear I saw made my heart feel like it would beat out of my chest.

"Sasha what happened to April?"

She looked at me with tears in her eyes.

"April…April…" she stammered.

I took a deep breath and released it before I spoke.

"Sasha, calm down and breathe."

She took several deep breaths. I knew something bad had happened. I've never seen Sasha so choked up. Once she was composed enough to speak, she told me what happened.

"April found a dead body in the back by the dumpsters."

I exhaled the breath I had no clue I'd been holding. It was a relief hearing April found the body and wasn't the body. I couldn't imagine losing her. Then it hit me. Someone else had been was dead.

"Where is April?" I asked.

She pointed to a police patrol car. The door was ajar and I saw April sitting inside with a blanket around her shoulders. I needed to get to her. I pushed through the group of people and past two police officers.

"April!" I called.

When she saw me, she ran from the car into my arms. She began to sob. I just held her. Out of nowhere Luciano appeared carrying a cup in his hands.

"I brought her some water," he said.

April pulled herself from me. She grabbed the cup and took a few sips. I clasped her hand and led her back over to the police car where she was sitting. I gave her a few minutes to calm down before prying information out of her.

"April, what happened?"

"Oh, Kim. It was terrible. There was blood everywhere."

She began to sob again. I rubbed her knee. She took another sip of water. Then continued.

"Kim, Ashley is dead."

I had to look like a deer in headlights. *Ashley was dead?* For some reason I started to shake.

"What happened?' I asked again.

"Well, Ashley asked me to go in on a client with her. Since Wendy's gone, she needed someone to help with her female clients. I really didn't want to, but the money sounded really nice."

I noticed a few more police cars pull up. I looked around at the scene. Then my eyes made contact with the same detective on Wendy's case. I averted my eyes and focused on April again.

"I told her I had a client and I would come looking for her when I was done. So I finished up, took a shower and searched for her."

Just then I saw a familiar scene. The coroner leading a body from the back of the building on a stretcher in a black zipped up body bag. It brought me back to my first day at work at this place. I shuddered. I turned away. April saw the same thing and began to cry again. It hit home that this was the fourth woman to die since I started working here.

"Kim, I was asking around for her and someone told me she went toward the back offices. Some of the women take Luciano's keys and go back to the alley to smoke a cigarette. I assumed that was where she went and that is when…when…I found her."

She began to cry again.

"Look, you don't have to talk about it anymore." I assured her.

Suddenly, we were interrupted.

"Excuse me Miss Lawson."

I turned around and came face to face with Detective Marshall.

"What can I do for you detective?"

"Can we speak in private?" he asked.

I knew what he wanted and I had no plan to speak with him. It had to do with my fight with Ashley. It wasn't lost on me I fought with Wendy and Ashley and they both ended up dead. I decided I would take Kenneth's advice.

"I can't speak to you without my attorney present." I replied.

He raised an eyebrow. "Why would you need an attorney? An innocent person doesn't need an attorney."

I knew he was trying to bait me.

"Look," I told him. "You have my attorney's number. Call him!"

I grabbed April.

"Let's go home. You need to rest and if they need you they know where to find you."

I walked her to my car and led her away from the lights, chaos and death.

When we arrived at our house, a familiar car was parked in the driveway. I pulled past it into the garage. I helped a still shaken April out and into the house. Then I approached the occupied vehicle. As I reached the driver side door, it opened and out stepped Kenneth.

"What are you doing here?"

After my talk with Malcolm, I was feeling uneasy about seeing Kenneth. I wasn't ready to confront him about the new information I had or whether to inform him about my past situation with his brother.

"I came by to see you. Then I got a call from Luciano and he told me everything."

My mind was still focused on what Malcolm told me. "Why did you come by to see me?"

He smiled and pulled me into his arms.

"Why wouldn't I?"

"We didn't have a date. You didn't call."

He frowned. "I didn't think I had to."

I didn't feel as safe in his arms as I used to. I pulled away and fixed my shirt. I felt guilty for feeling that way. I knew Malcolm was trying to get me back in his bed. He could have lied and told me anything to get me away from Kenneth. But I would be lying if I didn't admit… it bothered me.

I looked toward the house and back at him.

"I should probably get in there. April is still pretty traumatized about what she saw."

"Want me to come with you?" he asked moving toward the house.

I placed my hand on his chest. "NO!"

He looked bewildered.

"I mean, it's probably best if I just…yeah." I said patting him on the chest.

I tried not to let what Malcolm said get to me. Yet as I walked into the house and left Kenneth standing in my driveway, it weighed heavily on my mind.

CHAPTER 30

Kimberly

Loud winds tore through the city as an unexpected storm pummeled the outside with rain. I sat in the corner of the coffee shop, laptop in front of me, trying to think about what I should do. The turmoil outside was equivalent to the pain I felt in my soul.

After Malcolm came over, I was feeling uncomfortable regarding my relationship with Kenneth. Some of the things he told me were disturbing and perplexing. I was having a hard time with Malcolm's threats and the information Kenneth stalked and harassed women. At first I thought, that wasn't the Kenneth I knew. It was then I realized...I didn't really know him. It had only been a month since we started seeing each other.

Every little thing he did once, I learned about his past had me on edge. After Ashley's death, I didn't really talk to anyone. I tried to avoid people from the lounge except April and Sasha. That didn't stop Kenneth from calling and texting me 20 times a day, every day for about a week. I had to block his number just so I could get some peace.

It had me worried.

I thought back to the way he pursued me with gifts and visits to the lounge. The very first time he requested me he said he wanted me. I saw him as a sweet guy trying to court me but…could there be more?

"Medium triple chocolate mocha?" the server interrupted my thoughts.

I nodded and he sat my drink down on the table in front of me.

"Thank you." I replied.

He smiled and walked away.

I took a sip and leaned back in my seat.

I knew that I was playing with fire seeing Kenneth. April told me never to get involved with a client. I didn't listen. There was no way I could continue to see him with Malcolm on my ass. The fact that Malcolm was a client of mine as well, only made things worse. It was all just too much. What was I thinking?

I guess, I thought that once I quit the lounge my relationship with Kenneth would go smoother. However, I failed to realize Kenneth was a part of that life. I was done with *Inferno* and I knew that would mean me being done with Kenneth as well.

I tried to shake off my emotions and focus on the task at hand. Trying to find a new job. I was on my laptop, oblivious to the world and trying to clean up my resume, when someone rapped on my table. I jumped, startled at the intrusion. I looked up and came face to face with Kenneth.

My eyes widened at the sight of him.

"Hi to you too," he said laughing.

I looked him up and down. I noticed the water dripping from his coat and on his face.

"You're soaked." I replied.

He chuckled.

"Yeah, it's chaos out there," he said taking the chair across from me. He took off his jacket and placed it on the back of his seat.

"How did you know I was here?" I questioned.

The only person who knew I was out was April and even then I didn't tell her exactly where.

"I stopped by your house and April told me you were going to a coffee shop. I checked all of the coffee shops in your area until I found your car."

It unnerved me that in this weather he checked at least seven coffee shops near my house just to find me.

"Why did you go through all that trouble?"

He smiled.

"Well, you haven't been responding to my phone calls and texts. I just wanted to make sure you were okay."

I softened a little. He was just looking out for me. I shouldn't be so bothered by him. I guess Malcolm succeeded in making me feel put off by Kenneth's affection. I felt a little guilty. But, I knew it wouldn't keep me from distancing myself. It was something that had to be done.

"Why aren't you at home? It's a mess outside," he said.

I cocked my head to the side. "I could ask you the same thing."

"I wanted to see your beautiful face," he said moving from the chair and coming over to sit next to me on the booth bench.

I averted my eyes trying not to fall for his charm.

"I just needed to get out of the house," I answered taking a sip of my drink. "I'm looking for jobs so I can continue to pay for school and my half of the rent."

He sat his elbow on the table and turned to face me.

"I was thinking about that."

"Thinking about what?" I asked.

"I was wondering what you would do once you left *Inferno*," he said placing his hand on my knee. "I have a solution for you."

I raised one eyebrow and folded my arms across my chest.

"And what is that?"

He scooted closer and leaned in.

"Why don't you move in with me?"

I was thrown by his words. It was way too early in our relationship to even think about moving in together.

"Kenneth, that's crazy."

He frowned at me. "Why? You wouldn't have to worry about rent. It's something I want to do."

I shifted in my seat. He was getting too close too soon and that worried me.

"But why?" I asked. "Why would you do that for me? You don't even know me."

"I know everything I need to know about you," he replied.

I sighed. His head was so in the clouds he couldn't see reality. I knew it was time that I walked away before I was caught up in his rose colored world.

"Kenneth, I think we need to take a break."

He raised an eyebrow.

"Okay, you don't have to move in with me. We can figure something else out…"

"No, we can't. You are moving too fast. I just need time to myself to figure this all out."

"I can help you?"

This wasn't going to be easy.

"You say you know everything you need to know about me. But, do I know everything I need to know about you?" I asked.

His brow was furrowed and his eyes narrowed.

"I don't know what you mean by that," he said.

I swallowed the lump in my throat. I had no clue how he would respond once I told him what I knew and how I knew it. But, he needed to know the truth. No matter what happened, he needed to know.

"Kenneth, I heard you were accused of stalking women. Is that true?"

His eyes widened, and then narrowed. Then he sighed.

"Yes," was his simple answer.

Malcolm wasn't lying!

I didn't fault Kenneth for not telling me. We hadn't been together long enough for those type of skeletons to come out of the closet. It only solidified my decision in my mind, however.

"How did you hear about that?' he questioned.

Maybe if he knew about Malcolm and me, he would see where I was coming from. He would see that a relationship between us would be so complicated it would be almost impossible to hold together.

"Malcolm told me."

There was a frown on his face. I knew he had to wonder why I would be talking to Malcolm about things so personal.

"Why would my brother tell you that?"

I took a deep breath then let it out. I placed my hand on his knee hoping to soften the blow.

"Malcolm…well…" I stammered.

"What?" he asked eagerly.

"Malcolm, well, he was one of my clients at *Inferno*."

His face went blank. I couldn't tell what he was thinking. We were both quiet for a minute. The only sounds were the chatter in the shop and the noise of the machines making the latest and most complicated coffee drinks.

Finally he spoke.

"Are you saying my brother cheated on his wife with you?"

I raised an eyebrow.

"Not just with me. He was sleeping with women at the lounge well before I started working there. Ashley was his main girl for years."

He turned to me and I finally saw some emotion on his face. Shock and surprise outlined his features. His eyes were enlarged. Then he was cool again. He took a deep inhale and exhaled it out slowly.

I decided I needed to complete my story.

"He was my client for awhile. Then he came to my house the other day asking for more. He wanted me to be his mistress. When I declined his offer, he told me he knew it was because of you and that is when he told me those things..."

He didn't look at me anymore. He just stared straight ahead. I decided not to say anything else until he spoke. I had said all I could say anyway. Now that the truth was out in the open I felt...relieved?

Finally he looked at me. His jaw was clenched. I could tell he was livid. I just didn't know if he was angry with me or his brother.

"Why didn't you tell me all this before?" he asked.

I ran my fingers through my braids.

"I didn't know how to tell you."

"So you break up with me then tell me?"

I realized he was angry with me. He removed my hand from his knee.

"Is my brother the VIP that requested you?"

I nodded.

He stood without saying another word. He grabbed his jacket and put it on. Then he spoke.

"I'll take care of this, Kim."

"Kenneth..."

"NO!" he yelled. I jumped in my seat. Other patrons in the coffee shop began to look our way.

The anger that runs in that family is scary, I thought.

"Kim, what we have between us isn't over," he insisted. "You can't just walk away. I won't let you."

I didn't want him to do anything. I just wanted to be liberated from it all. It was stressful and draining and I just wanted to be free. I cared about Kenneth, but I felt my independence from *Inferno* was paramount.

"Kenneth, just let this go. Let me go."

He shook his head. He breathed through flared nostrils before he spoke.

"I'll fix this. I'm going to have a little talk with my brother."

He took a step closer to me.

"Then I'll handle you."

With that, he walked away and out of the coffee shop.

I didn't know what he meant by "handle" me but I had to admit. I was afraid.

CHAPTER 31

Malcolm

"These fucking cameras better give me some answers." Tony leaned in staring at the monitors.

I agreed. The lounge had already lost a few clients once the cameras were installed and for them not to give us clues would be devastating and a waste of time. I was right thinking the new security guards would deter a killer from attacking upstairs. But, it didn't stop him. We were all wrong believing it would deter someone from killing at all.

Tony and I sat in the back office we turned into a command center for all the video footage. There were wall to wall monitors so we could keep an eye on every angle of the club except for the VIP rooms.

After Ashley's murder, the police raided the place. They found this room and demanded all the video we had. Tony understood that if it got out he turned tapes over to the cops it would be the end of *Inferno*. So we lied. We lied and used the officers we had on the payroll to say that the cameras were either not working or had no tapes. We continued to lie and say any video we did have was useless.

Of course they didn't believe us. So, we ended up turning over some footage from the front of the building claiming those were the only cameras that worked. That seemed to satisfy them. Tony knew that could still do some damage to the business. It had video of the people who came and left from the lounge. That made him more determined to catch the killer. We had been watching video footage of the night Ashley died for a few hours now hoping we would see something or find something that would point us to a possible suspect.

We were alone in the room which was a first. Whenever I met with Tony, he was always surrounded by security or body guards. I guess I was the only one he trusted to see what was on those tapes.

I didn't feel honored.

The death of Ashley left a bad taste in my mouth. Not because I cared what happened to her. Having her dead actually helped me out. She could no longer blackmail me if she were six feet under. No, it was the way she was murdered that got to me. According to Sasha, April came running in screaming from the back. Sasha was the first one to grab her and make her talk. It wasn't easy. She was hysterical. That is when she blurted out that Ashley was dead. She told Sasha and some clients where to find her. They all raced to the alley and found Ashley's bloody body. I was told it was a horrendous sight. Blood everywhere.

They tried looking for Luciano and Tony but couldn't find them. Before they had a chance to get a hold of them, someone called the police. Once they arrived there was only so much I could do.

Her death affected Tony in a different way. It meant the lounge was again closed. He was a mess about that. He insisted we watch hours and hours of video tape looking for any clues. We searched every inch of tape. Our main focus was the footage from the alley. The bad thing was one of the cameras, the one by the dumpster, wasn't working. It was dark in that area and the camera only picked up half of the alley closest to the front of the building.

After awhile, I barely paid attention to the monitors. After staring forever at uneventful footage, my mind drifted. It didn't help that my phone wouldn't stop ringing. My brother was calling. I refused to answer. I knew what he wanted. I'm sure by this time Kim has told him about my proposition. I knew he would be pissed. His temper wasn't something I wanted to deal with right now. In between the constant calls from my brother, I was texting Kim. She wasn't replying to my messages but I continued to send them. I needed to convince her to take me up on my offer. It was less about competing with my brother and more about having Kim.

I didn't know what was happening to me but she was occupying my mind with thoughts of fucking her.

"Malcolm! Fucking focus!" Tony exclaimed. "Between your phone ringing or the clicking of your cell as you text, I can't concentrate."

I went through my phone settings and put my phone on 'do not disturb'. I placed it back in my pocket. I tried to focus on the videotape again.

I didn't mention this to Tony, but I was convinced Abigail didn't kill Sarah. I believed we had a serial killer on our hands. I met with a few police officers and they gave me some new information. Wendy also had Xanax and sleeping pills in her system and the medical examiner determined her death was a homicide. What was worse, it seemed like this killer was escalating. He went from drugging and killing to stabbing. The thought that someone was murdering women in *Inferno* had me freaked out. I knew if I gave Tony this information he would flip out as well. That would help no one. I just hoped this latest murder of Ashley would lead us to the killer. Maybe he slipped up and made a mistake we could take advantage of.

"Did you see that?" Tony asked me.

I squinted my eyes and tried to focus on the grainy video footage from the alley.

"Why couldn't you shell out a few more bucks to get some better cameras out there?" I asked.

He turned to glare at me.

"We already had cameras in the alley. I didn't see the need to update them."

I shook my head. My eyes went back to the monitors. I watched as Tony rewound the tape. He pressed play when he saw something suspicious.

"Look at that," he said touching the screen.

It was then that I saw the cuts on his hands.

"Where did you get those?" I inquired. "Those cuts look really deep."

"Malcolm," he said. "Focus! Look!"

I refocused on the screen in front of me. You could barely make out a person limping down the alley toward the front of the building.

"Is that Ashley?" I asked.

"I have no clue." Tony replied.

We continued watching as the person fell hitting the ground. Then another figure appeared. Because of the terrible picture, you couldn't make out what either person looked like. It was dark and slightly blurry. You could tell, however, one person was dragging the other down the alley by the legs out of the view of the working camera.

"Oh shit!" I exclaimed.

I was convinced at that moment we had just witnessed Ashley's murder.

"Oh shit, is right." Tony said leaning back in his chair. "What do we do with this?" he asked.

I knew this was something we should turn over to the police. There was a chance they had equipment that could enhance the tape and possibly ID the perpetrator. This, if they were able do something with the footage, could blow the case wide open.

"Tony, this…," I said pointing toward the screen. "could be explosive! They could possible use it to identify the killer. We should turn this over to the police."

He shook his head.

"I don't agree Malcolm. We've already told them we have no more tapes. How will it look now that we've uncovered more? They may get a warrant to search for the rest of what we have or worse."

He had a point. I knew his biggest fear was a threat the detective made. He warned us he would get a warrant for the names of the members of the lounge. That would close down *Inferno* for good. Yet I knew they would be more grateful to have this grainy video then to really care if we had more. We could hide the rest and tell them we overlooked a camera. It would appear we were fully cooperating by turning it over.

"Tony, we need to turn this over to the police."

He ran his fingers through his hair and looked over at me.

"Look, I think we should keep this under wraps. I want to catch this son-of-a bitch as much as anybody else. His murder spree is costing me money. However, I think this video would do more harm than good."

"Then we turn it over to the cops on the payroll. They can determine if it would help or not and…"

"NO!" he yelled.

At that moment we heard a banging at the door. It was one of those "it's the police and we have a warrant" type bangs. Tony scrambled to grab all the tapes and turn off the monitors. When he was done, I stood and went for the door. Once I opened it, I really wished I hadn't. I sighed.

"Malcolm, we need to talk." Kenneth said.

CHAPTER 32

Kimberly

The wind and rain smacked against my bedroom window. I closed my eyes and focused on my pleasure.

After seeing Kenneth, I left the café unnerved, miserable and very aware of my sexual frustration. Seeing him made me realize how much I wanted him. That made me sad. I knew there was a chance I may never touch him again. His brother and my own fear of being with him would see to that.

Yet, being near him turned me on so much. I barely made it through the door before I was in the room, climbing into bed and touching myself.

I slowly ran my hands up and down my legs. They traveled up until they reached the meeting between my thighs caressing my sex. Adjusting myself on the bed, I moaned. I put two fingers inside and pulled them out. I found my g-spot and stroked myself there. In and out they went bringing me closer. Using my thumb to caress my clit, I pushed in and pulled out.

I shuddered as I hit the right spot. Staying there, I brought myself to climax. I came hard against my fingers. But I didn't stop. I continued to stroke myself.

My breathing was heavy. Feeling my orgasm build, I came again. Not as hard as the first orgasm but still leaving me breathless.

I lay there savoring the pleasure. I felt clearer in my thoughts and contemplated calling Kenneth. I didn't like how we left things. My plan wasn't to break up with him like that. I wanted to let him down gently.

Suddenly, I heard the doorbell. I was reluctant to answer. It was 12 am and I wasn't expecting anyone. Maybe it was Kenneth. He could have come by to talk. He did say he would handle me after he dealt with Malcolm.

I'm not in the mood to be handled.

I ignored the doorbell until there was a pounding at the door. I sighed and rolled my body out of the bed. I dressed and headed down the hall to the front door.

I looked out of the peep hole and was surprised at who I saw standing on my front porch. I unlocked the myriad of locks April had installed and opened the door. Standing there staring at his shoes and wringing his hands was Luciano. When he saw me he smiled.

"Hi beautiful," he said.

"Hey Luc," I said stepping out of the way letting him enter. "What brings you by here, in this downpour?"

He sat his dripping umbrella outside against the house and wiped his shoes on the mat before he entered. Once he was inside, I relocked the door.

"I came by to see you. Check up on you," he said shedding himself of his damp coat and laying it across the arm of the recliner.

Luciano was sweet like that. He was different from a lot of the men that worked or frequented the club. I was sure he had been going around checking up on all the girls. I felt like I could be honest with him so I let loose a multitude of complaints.

"It's just so frustrating. I can't find a job," I said walking over and plopping down on the couch. "Then there is Kenneth and Malcolm. I just can't emotionally or mentally deal with either of them right now."

He came to sit down next to me. He placed his hand on my knee.

"It's okay. I didn't just come over empty handed. I came with solutions," he announced.

I raised an eyebrow. I had a feeling he was going to request I start taking clients again.

"Luc, I'm done being a companion. I can't do that anymore…"

He shook his head vigorously.

"I'm not going to suggest you do that anymore," he said.

He moved closer.

"My solution involves you and I helping each other."

He ran his hand through his hair. It was then that I noticed the large stitched up scar on his head. I ran my finger across it.

"Where did you get this? Kenneth has a similar one on his head. You both must be some clumsy people."

He laughed.

"Yes, I'm pretty clumsy. I fell and hit my head on the kitchen counter. It hurt like hell."

"I bet!" I responded.

"Let me finish," he said. "I want us to help each other."

I had no clue what he meant.

"How can we do that?"

His hand moved from my knee to my upper thigh.

"We could go back to the arrangement we had before. You know," he said cocking his head to the side. "I go down on you and then pay you whatever you want me to."

The large smile on his face gave me the impression he was confident I would accept his offer.

For a second I almost entertained the idea. My job hunt had been going nowhere. Once I paid spring tuition I would be absolutely broke. It would also solve my issue with the Johnson brothers. If I started having sex with Luciano, Kenneth would know I wasn't going back to him and Malcolm would be off my case.

As quickly as those thoughts flashed through my mind, I rejected them. I was done with that lifestyle. Plus, I wasn't quite sold on my decision to leave Kenneth. Malcolm be damned! Though I broke up with Kenneth, my heart was still wanting to be with him and be held in his arms.

I removed Luciano's hand from my leg and moved over putting some space between us.

"Luc, I'm sorry but that isn't going to work for me."

He reached into his back pocket and pulled out his wallet.

I sighed.

"I can offer you more if you want…"

"Luc," I said placing my hand on his wallet. "Put that away. No amount of money is going to make me change my mind."

His smile disappeared and was replaced with a look I had never seen before. His eyebrows were furrowed, his eyes were narrowed, nostrils were flared and his lips were pursed together. He seemed…angry?

Just as fast as the expression was there, it was gone and he was smiling.

"Let's have a drink," he said standing and heading for the kitchen.

"Isn't it too late to be drinking?" I asked looking at my watch. 12:36 am.

He laughed.

"You've had a drink later than this at *Inferno*. You can have just one drink with me tonight."

I sighed. He was right. Plus with all that was going on in my life, a drink didn't really sound bad.

"I know April has a ton of alcohol somewhere in this house. She drinks like a frat boy at the lounge," he quipped.

I laughed.

I walked over to the upper cabinet in the corner by the refrigerator and threw it open.

"Ta-da!" I exclaimed.

There before us was a plethora of different types of alcohol beverages and mixers.

"There is also cranberry juice, orange juice and soda in the refrigerator."

He laughed and shook his head.

"I'm going to use this grenadine, green apple vodka and make you something special," he said pulling bottles out of the cabinet.

"The cups are next to that cabinet," I said.

He opened the door to the right and removed two glasses.

He whistled while he mixed drinks. I thought it was adorable. It made me think about how someone so thoughtful and sweet would be working at *Inferno* for the Santinos. I guess the money he made was a great incentive to put up with their bullshit. Yet he was incredibly smart and intelligent. April told me he had a MBA in Accounting and Finance. Apparently he used to be a high paid CPA for some very rich people. He could be living a lucrative, quiet life somewhere with a wife and kids not working in a sleazy night club and sleeping with the escorts.

"Here we are. Vodka, grenadine and lemon-lime soda."

I didn't know if that was a winning combination but he seemed confident that mix would work. He walked over to me. I reached for a glass and he moved it handing me the other. I immediately took a sip of my drink. It was strong and had a bitter after taste.

"Whoa," I said "are you trying to knock me out?"

He smiled.

"Exactly," he said laughing.

He sat his drink down on the table and came to stand behind me.

"You seem tense, let me help you with that," he said.

I felt the weight of his hands on my shoulders as he began to massage them. I took another sip of my drink. I guess it wasn't too terrible. The lemon-lime soda helped to combat some of the bitterness. He continued to rub and knead my shoulders. Then his hands moved closer to my neck. His rubbing became deeper and more intense.

"How do you feel?" he asked.

I had to admit. I was feeling a little looser. My eyes felt heavy and his massaging of my neck only made me more relaxed.

"You're good at this," I replied taking another sip of my drink.

"I know," he said. "I'm good at pleasing women."

Suddenly our little party was intruded upon by April bursting through the door leading inside from the garage. When she spotted Luciano and me in the kitchen she stopped. When Luciano saw April he backed away from me.

"Hey guys! What are you two up to?" she asked walking over to us.

"Well, umm…" Luciano stammered. "Well, Kim was feeling a little stressed so we decided to have a drink."

"It looked like more than having drinks to me," she said smiling.

"Trust me," I said chuckling. "That's all that was going on. I am done with that life, remember?"

She shook her head and laughed. Then I watched as she grabbed my drink and turned it up robbing the entire glass of its liquid.

"That was pretty good," she said.

"It wasn't a little bitter?" I asked.

She shook her head. "It was fine to me."

Maybe I was more of a light weight than I had previously thought. In fact, I was feeling a little heavy. My eyes started to droop. I knew I must be getting tired. It had been a long day. I tried to fight off the feelings and focus on April.

I noticed tonight must be a working night for her. She was wearing a short leather skirt and a tight red tank top with a low swooping V-neck.

"You have a client tonight?" I asked focusing intently on my breathing.

She nodded.

"Yes, but I left some of my costumes at the lounge. I have to go and pick those up first."

I sighed.

I hated that April was still working as an escort. Despite promising me she would quit working until the killer was caught, she continued to have sex for money. "How am I supposed to cover my half of the bills and your half of the bills if I don't work?" she asked me. I didn't have a good answer. It had been over a couple of decades since she has done anything different and it would be unlikely she would find a job that would give her the lifestyle she was accustomed to.

So I didn't rag on her for going out tonight.

"Why did you come home if your stuff is at the lounge?"

She came over and wrapped her arms around me.

"I was hoping you could give me a ride to the lounge. My client is meeting me there and my check engine light came on. I have no idea what's going on and I don't want to drive it like that."

"I've been drinking April and I don't really feel all that well," I replied. "You know if it wasn't for that I would drive you. Why don't you just take my car and bring it back to me in the morning?"

"Why don't I just give you a ride?" Luciano said. "I know Tony is at the lounge tonight. He may need my help with some things."

"Oh, Luc," she said moving from me and embracing him tightly. "That would be great. I wouldn't feel comfortable leaving Kim's car at the lounge overnight."

I was glad they were leaving. I wasn't feeling all that well. I stood and carried myself to the living room and lay across the couch. I heard them whispering to each other or they could have been talking normally. I wouldn't know. I was too far gone to understand what they were saying. I closed my heavy eyelids and passed out right there.

CHAPTER 33

Kenneth

The rain was relentless. The wet pavement made it difficult to see the lines on the road. That made me anxious. Anxiety mixed with anger and frustration was a bad combination. My head ached and my heart raced.

I left the café with Kim seething. I called my brother's house and found out he wasn't home to the frustration of his wife. I headed straight for *Inferno* planning to have a little chat with him. I knew he would be there. *Where else would he be?*

I planned to confront Malcolm about the information Kim gave me. When I heard she and my brother slept together, my body and mind was ravaged with shock, anger and dismay. Not only was Malcolm throwing away the best thing in his life –his family- for a quick fix, but he was also asking the woman I loved to be his mistress.

I was livid.

It's not like I cared who Kim slept with before me. I knew what she did for a living. I'm not an idiot. But I would be lying if I said it didn't bother me knowing one of her clients was my brother.

Despite my anger, I wasn't going to let Kim dump me. I knew she didn't really want to throw what we had away. I could see it in her big brown eyes. I just needed to get Malcolm and Tony out of the way. Once I did that, we could be together in peace.

I arrived at *Inferno* and dashed from my car to the front entrance, pummeled by quarter sized raindrops along the way. By the time I swung open the door and entered I was soaked.

I immediately began my search for Malcolm. I searched offices and even VIP rooms. There was no sight of him or anyone else for that matter. It was weird seeing the lounge so empty this late into the night. At this hour, it was normally bustling with activity.

The death of Ashley forced Tony to officially close until the killer was found. I knew this had to upset him. He would be missing out on money. Making money was the most important thing to him. The safety of the women working here was secondary.

I returned to the main room to find Sasha at the bar wiping up the counter and organizing martini and whiskey glasses on a high shelf.

Where was she when I first entered?

"What are you doing here?" I asked.

She jumped when she heard my voice and dropped the glass she was holding. The sound of a shattering tumbler echoed throughout the place.

She turned to me and glared.

"God, Kenneth!" she exclaimed. "You scared the shit out of me!"

I rushed over. I dropped down in front of her and began to pick up the larger pieces of glass. I carefully tossed them in the trash. She grabbed a small brush and dust pan and swept up the remaining smaller pieces.

"I really didn't mean to scare you. I was just wondering with the lounge closed, why you were here?"

She stood with her hand on her hip.

"Probably the same reason you're here. Just can't stay away from this place."

I laughed and shook my head.

"Actually, I'm here looking for Malcolm. I looked around the empty room. "I'm under the assumption he's not here."

Sasha shook her head.

"Oh, he's here," she said leaning against the bar. "He and Tony have been holed up for hours in the security camera room."

I folded my arms across my chest.

"Security camera room? When did they get that?" I asked.

"When they put in all those," she said pointing to a camera in the corner.

"Where is this room?" I asked.

Sasha, moving from behind the bar, grabbed my arm and led me to the back hall.

"It's the last room on your right by the back door." Then she left me alone to face my brother and Tony on my own.

I had no clue those offices were being used. After Sarah was found dead in one of those rooms, no one ventured back there. I followed Sasha's instructions and arrived at the last entrance on the right. I could feel my anger rising as I approached.

I banged on the door. No one came. So I knocked again. Finally the door swung open and there stood my brother.

"Malcolm, we need to talk." I said.

He sighed.

He stepped out of the room and closed the door behind him.

"Come on Ken, let's go by the bar and talk there."

He didn't wait for me. He headed down the hall. I watched as he turned out of sight.

Then I followed.

I reached the main lounge area and found him sitting on one of the couches. I walked over and took a seat in front of him. He leaned back on the sofa and folded his arms across his chest.

"What can I do for you?" he asked nonchalantly.

His blasé approach made my anger resurface. I leaned in placing my elbows on my knees and my chin on my hands.

"Well," I began. "Kim told me a very interesting story. I'm just here to hear your side."

He raised an eyebrow.

"I can't read your mind Ken. Are you going to tell me what she said or are we going to play the guessing game."

I took in a deep breath and let it out before I spoke.

"She told me about your involvement with her, Ashley, and other women at this club."

He rolled his eyes. "You came all this way, in this storm, to confront me about some whores at the club? Really Ken?"

His attitude was pissing me off. I took a deep breath and tried to mimic his calm.

I ignored his question.

"I guess you're not denying anything. That's disappointing."

He leaned forward and glared at me."Disappointed? You're disappointed in me?"

I could tell my displeasure bothered him.

"You tell me the girls at the club are no good and I'm better off without them. Then I find out you're here cheating on your wife with them," I said.

"It's not like I lied to you. These women ARE no good and you ARE better off without them."

"Really?" I asked chuckling at his nerve.

"Yes," he said. "There is a difference between you and me, Ken. I can have casual sex with these women and still have a family. You want to marry these women. These sluts aren't wife material."

I shook my head in disbelief.

"You call them whores, sluts and bitches but you're sleeping around with them. Does Evelyn know? I'm sure she would like to know…"

That did the trick. He stood. I stood as well. His face was no longer blank but full of expression. His eyes narrowed and his hands balled into fist. I took a large step forward toward him until we were only inches apart.

I wanted him as angry as I was and bringing Evelyn into this conversation seemed to work.

"Are you planning to blackmail me? Your own brother?" he asked. "Are you planning to tell Evelyn ? Because that may not be a good idea little brother."

"Leave Kim alone and no one has to know about you or anything else you do."

His nostrils flared and his breathing increased.

"I don't appreciate being threatened or you bringing my wife into this."

"You brought this on yourself." I responded.

Suddenly Sasha came over. She put a hand on each of our chests and pushed us apart.

"Look, I don't want to get in the middle of this…"

"Too late," Malcolm said.

She rolled her eyes. "Remember you two are brothers. You shouldn't let anything come between you."

"Thanks Sasha for your unsolicited advice."

"Malcolm, stop being an asshole."

He laughed.

The fact that he thought this was all fun and games fueled my fury. He didn't care about anything or anyone but himself.

"Look, I'm leaving. Do you think you boys can keep your hands to yourself while I'm gone?"

"Sasha, we'll be fine," he said.

She looked at me. My brow was furrowed and my nostrils were flared. My hands were clinched into fist and my eyes were narrowed. She knew I wasn't going to make the same promise.

She sighed.

I watched her walk over and grab her purse off the bar. She headed out the front entrance. I heard the click of the locks. My attention was brought back to my brother.

"Look, Ken," he said placing his hand on my shoulder. "Sasha is right. We're brothers. We shouldn't be arguing over some ho'."

I knocked his hand off me.

"She's not some ho'."

He shook his head.

"Kenneth, that's exactly what she is."

"She's more than that."

He sighed.

"Why can't you see what's right in front of your face. You can't build a life with a prostitute, an escort, a companion, or a stripper. Why can't you leave these girls alone and find someone more wholesome?"

I'm not even sure he realized how hypocritical and absurd his words were. He was practically throwing his family away for these girls. If Evelyn ever found out, life as he knew it would be over. Yet he stood here lecturing me.

"But you want her to be your mistress," I said.

"Yes. I want her to be my mistress. A mistress. Not my wife or a girlfriend."

I knew my anger was close to erupting. I needed to get away from my brother. But, before I did, I had to make one thing clear.

"Malcolm, stay away from Kim. We are trying to build something together and the last thing we need is you trying to get in her pants."

"I'll do what I want to do and I'll fuck who I want to fuck," he callously replied.

I took a step toward him until I could smell his breath.

I lowered my voice.

"If you don't leave Kim alone, Evelyn will hear all about *Inferno*."

"Don't threaten me, Ken," he said pushing me backward. "Kim doesn't want you. She's just like the rest. She's going to drop you and take me up on my offer. Women like that value money over love. There is no way she cares about you. She will dump you and end up on my payroll."

I thought about Kim dumping me in the coffee shop. Was my brother right? Did Kim dump me so she could service my brother? No. That can't be it. Kim wanted out of this world. She didn't really want to let me go.

"Malcolm, for the last time," I said clinching and releasing my fist over and over again. "You and Tony need to back off and let Kim go."

"Just give it up, Ken. She doesn't want you and she'll never want you."

My rage overcame me and without much thought, I lunged at him. To our surprise, the chair he was standing in front of fell backwards under our weight and we spilled out onto the floor.

CHAPTER 34

Kimberly

Boom!

Thunder rumbled throughout the house. I jolted upward on the couch. My eyes tried to adjust to the darkness all around. The only other thing that could be heard was the ringing of a phone somewhere.

My mind was still a little foggy and my head had a dull ache. It took me a minute to realize I was completely alone. I had no clue how I had gotten that way. My last memory was of Luciano and April discussing taking her back to the lounge to collect some of her belongings.

I sat up completely and rubbed my eyes with the palms of my hands. The ringing in the house ceased and was replaced by an eerie silence. I looked at my watch. 3:36am. I had been out at least a couple of hours.

I jumped as the ringing started up again and a strike of lightening temporarily illuminated the darkness. I rose from the couch and followed the ringing. It led me into the kitchen. I flicked the switch and the darkness was snuffed out and replaced by the bright light of the 14 watt halogen bulb.

I continued to follow the noise. I finally found it on the kitchen table just as the ringing stopped.

I realized that the phone didn't belong to me. I turned it over in my hands and realized it wasn't April's either. I deduced that the last person in our house was Luciano and the phone must belong to him. He probably left it in his mad dash to drop off April. I wondered if he realized it was missing. I decided he knew where he was last and would come here looking for it. There was no need to fret about it.

Suddenly it began to ring in my hand again. I didn't plan on answering it but when I saw the number I changed my mind. It was April's number. What if she needed Luciano for something and I had his phone?

"Hello?"

The voice I heard on the other end of the phone was not April's but a male's.

"Kim, you're awake. Thank goodness."

Luciano's voice poured through the speaker.

"Yeah, I just woke up." I said. "I guess you realized you left your phone at my house."

He chuckled. "Yeah, I was looking all over for it and remembered I took it out of my pocket and set it down somewhere."

I leaned against the counter. "Where is April? I thought she had a client. How did you end up with her phone?"

"April? Well, she let me borrow her phone to call you. She is in the bathroom."

I raised an eyebrow.

"So when are you coming to pick it up?"

He sighed.

"That's the problem. Tony has me working here all night. I doubt if he is going to let me leave anytime soon."

I furrowed my brow.

"I thought the lounge was closed," I said.

"It is," he responded. "There is still tons of paperwork that needs to be sorted out."

I pursed my lips together. *There was always something with that place. The police need to shut it down for good*, I thought.

"Kim, I really need my phone."

I sighed.

I knew what he wanted me to do. I really wasn't in the mood to venture out into the storm. I walked to the window above the kitchen sink that looked out into the backyard. You could see some lightening, but there wasn't much rain falling anymore. I thought maybe I could run the phone up there and get back before the rain really got started again.

"Okay Luc, because you're always so good to me, I'll bring you your phone."

"Yes! Thank you. You're the best."

I ended the call and put the phone in the pocket of my jogging pants. Looked like I was heading to *Inferno,* the last place I wanted to be. My gut was telling me I needed to just stay away. I almost called Luciano back to say I changed my mind. I didn't. Throwing on a hoodie, I grabbed my purse and phone and headed out the door.

I could not explain it but I didn't feel right about driving to the lounge. It was more than just the dread of possibly seeing Malcolm. There was another feeling I could not place.

I made sure I drove carefully through the city. There were tree branches and power lines down in the streets and in many people's yards. It seemed like it took longer to get there than it normally did. I arrived and found more cars in the parking lot than I expected. The place was supposed to be closed but there were at least three cars in the lot. I recognized Malcolm's black Mercedes and Kenneth's red Kia Optima.

That made me worry. If they both were in the same place tonight…after what I told Kenneth, It couldn't be a pleasant conversation.

I hopped out of my car and ran toward the front entrance just as I felt a few raindrops hit my hands. I reached the door and pulled on the handle. Locked! Damn! I pulled out my cell and tried to call the landlines in the offices. Of course no one answered. With the placed being closed, there was no one to man those phones.

I remembered Luciano called me from April's cell phone. I tried calling her but she didn't answer. I guess she was finally with her client. I was frustrated. I came all this way and I couldn't get into the club. I wanted to use Luciano's phone to call someone that could get in touch with him, like Tony, but his phone was locked.

I decided to try banging on the door, maybe someone would answer. I approached the front door again and just as I was about to knock, there was a loud bang against it. I jumped back and placed my hand over my heart. It was beating rapidly. I was afraid of what was going on in there.

I decided Luciano was just going to have to deal with his phone tomorrow. I stepped away from the door. I began to walk back to my car when Luc's phone began to ring again. I pulled it from my pocket and saw it was a call from April's phone. That was weird. I answered anyway.

"Hello?"

"Hey," Luc said. "How much longer are you going to be?"

"I'm here," I informed him. "But the front door is locked."

I could hear rustling on the line then he spoke again.

"Come down the alley to the back door. I'll open it up for you," he said.

I felt tightness in my chest at the thought. Ashley was killed in that alley and I heard the police just removed the tape no longer making it a crime scene. I didn't feel comfortable going down there.

"I just can't go down that alley."

"I'll be at the back door to open it for you," he promised.

I sighed. "Okay, but you're sure you'll be there to get me?"

I didn't understand why he couldn't just come and open the front door and let me in. Against my better judgment I didn't ask. I didn't press him.

"Yes, dear," he said. "I'll be there to get you."

I hung up the phone. I took a deep breath and drug myself toward the club. I slowly and cautiously walked to the side of the building toward the alley.

The dips in the ground collected the rain creating large pools of water. I avoided them as I checked my surroundings traveling into the shadows. There was only one light at each end so most of the alley was dark.

I could only hear the thunder and drops of rain falling from the eaves of the building. I continued my journey for the back door. When I got close I saw a heap of something near the doorway. I stopped in my tracks. *What was that?* Fear rippled through me for some reason and I took a few steps back. Then something inside of me said I needed to go forward and look closely at the strange mound.

Reluctantly I walked forward. As I got closer I saw it wasn't just a random pile. I could make out clothes. I could see a hand in a puddle. My eyes trained in on the red shirt. My mind began to bounce from one thought to another and the tightness in my chest felt like an invisible hand squeezing my lungs. I couldn't breathe. My feet felt as if they were glued to the spot.

I stared at the large emerald ring on the hand and knew exactly who I was looking at.

I screamed. That seemed to jolt my brain to action. Suddenly I was able to move and I rushed over to her.

"April!" I yelled.

She was lying on her stomach. Her body was in a spread eagle position and soaking wet. I shook her and she didn't move. I noticed a belt around her neck. It was pulled tight. I fought frantically to undo it.

"April, please wake up!"

I shook her again. She didn't budge. I pulled my phone from the front of my hoodie and with shaky hands I tried to call the police. I dropped my phone and it fell in the puddle next to April's hand. It was then I noticed blood.

I screamed again.

With tears pouring down my face, I picked up my phone and tried to dry it off quickly. I tried to turn it on. It came on but began to restart. "SHIT!" I yelled.

Hysterical and not sure what to do, I jumped up from the ground and began to bang on the back door.

"Help! Help!" I screamed.

I hammered on the door until my hands hurt like hell. No one came and so I tried my phone again. It was working! I began to dial when suddenly I was grabbed from behind. I dropped my cell phone and it broke into three different pieces.

A hand was placed on my mouth and something hard was shoved into my back. I went to scream. The object was pushed harder into me.

"If you scream, I'll just have to kill you," he warned.

CHAPTER 35

Malcolm

It was as if things were happening in slow motion.

The impact of the ground on the back of my head was painful. The shock threw me for a second. Kenneth grabbed me by the collar as he straddled me.

He swung to hit me and landed a blow to the side of my face. On his second try, despite the blows to my head, I was able to grab his wrist stopping the impact of his fist to my face again. He seemed surprised. His eyes widened and stared at my hand on him. I used that split second to roll us both over until I was on top.

With my head still radiating with pain, I tried to calm him down.

"Ken, this is not what you want." I said pinning him to the floor. I knew I was a little bit stronger than my brother. I lifted weights and worked out regularly. He was naturally thin. However, he had fury and adrenaline on his side. He struggled to free himself but I continued to hold him.

"Ken, knock it off!" I yelled.

He struggled a few more minutes until finally he seemed to calm down. Some of the fight in him seemed to have gone. I decided to release him in hopes we could talk about this.

I was wrong.

He seemed intent on punishing me. I didn't see him swing, but I felt the impact of his fist against my jaw. It was a surprisingly powerful punch that knocked me off him and to the side. He rolled over and came to me. I could see the cold hard look in his eyes. He wanted to beat the shit out of me.

I couldn't let him do that.

He swung again and I moved causing him to miss. We tussled for awhile rolling back and forth trying to get the better of the other. Until finally, I was able to climb to my feet. By this point, I was livid. My face hurt where he hit me, my head still ached from hitting the ground and the last thing I wanted to do was fight my brother over some woman.

He scrambled to his feet and faced me. He was standing there still ready for a fight. There was rage inside of him and it seemed he needed to release it somehow. I just needed to make sure I was no longer the target.

"Stop being an idiot, Ken!" I yelled.

He paced back and forth like an enraged animal locked in a cage. He kicked a chair over as he paced.

"I'm not being an idiot. I'm sick of you trying to run my life and telling me who I can or can't be with. You are a hypocritical piece of shit and I am tired of it."

I was offended by his words. I knew I wasn't perfect and I had my issues. But, a piece of shit?

I raised an eyebrow.

"I'm a piece of shit?" I asked. "And you think you're perfect?"

I pointed a finger at him.

"How many women have you stalked or harassed just to get what you want? You force women to be with you even when they don't want you. You don't think that makes you a piece of shit?"

He stalked toward me. My words struck a nerve. I knew that it would but I was angry and couldn't just let his insult go.

"I'm not the one cheating on my wife!" he exclaimed.

"No, maybe you're not. But, you're cheating yourself out of a good life. You don't need these women."

He took a step closer.

"I'm done with this conversation," He pointed his finger in my face. "I'm not going to say this again. Leave Kim alone!"

I shook my head. Not to tell him no, but in total disbelief. I couldn't believe my brother was willing to fight me over Kim. I didn't want to come to anymore blows with him but I refused to let him pursue her. It was what a big brother would do. I had to look out for him whether he liked it or not. If that meant beating some sense into him...then so be it!

I jumped back as he flung a black metal chair across the lounge. It landed against the front entrance door. The sound echoed throughout the place.

It was then that I knew knocking sense into him wasn't going to be easy. His anger, when it was at its peak, was a force I didn't want to tangle with.

Fighting wasn't going to work. We would both just end up battered and bruised.

"Ken, just settle down. We can talk this through. We should be able to calmly discuss this without battling."

He shook his head.

"The time for talk is over. I tried to convince you to leave her alone. I am done talking."

He came at me and I braced myself for a brutal assault.

Just as he reached me…we heard a scream come from the back offices. It stopped us both in our tracks.

"Did you hear that?" I asked Kenneth.

He slowly nodded his head.

Suddenly we heard a faint noise that sounded like drums in a marching band. It was a banging that reverberated throughout the lounge.

I knew Tony was back there reviewing the video tapes but this sounded like a woman's scream and the banging was frantic. Before I had a chance to completely process the situation, Kenneth was heading toward the back in a hurry.

"Ken what are you doing?" I asked.

He stopped and turned to me.

"I need to see what is going on. It sounds like someone is hurt or in danger."

Just like my brother to go running toward the chaos without thinking anything through.

"Wait, we have no clue what's going on. It could just be the tapes Tony is checking out," I said.

I had no reason to believe the scream would have come from the surveillance tapes but with a killer on the loose I didn't see why we should go running into danger.

"There is only one way to find out. I'm going to check it out," he announced.

Before I had a chance to stop him he was off running in the direction of the sound. I sighed.

I wasn't so sure that was a good idea.

But, I followed him anyway.

CHAPTER 36

The only sounds that could be heard was the sloshing of our feet in the puddles down the alley and the low rumble of thunder in the distance.

"I just have to get my things…"

Her voice slurred as she spoke and her right arm hung loosely across my shoulder. I was slightly annoyed at the woman leaning against me. I didn't plan to help her get her stuff. I only wanted her out of the way.

"We'll get your items, dear," I reassured her. "Just a few more steps to the back door."

She gripped me tighter as her heeled shoe hit a hole in the ground and she slipped.

Drugging her tonight wasn't part of the plan. But I would be an idiot if I didn't take advantage of the situation. I eyed her thick thighs and large breasts. Her plump luscious lips turned me on and I wondered why she and I had never been intimate.

She was probably like all the rest. Believing she was too good for me. Most of the women at the lounge felt that way. Except for one woman.

April wasn't who I really wanted. I knew Kim would give me the ultimate bliss. It had been a while since I had my hands around a woman's neck. I learned I couldn't feel pleasure any other way. My body yearned for the ecstasy I got when the life slowly drained from their bodies. The way they fought back, as I controlled whether they lived or died, enhanced the pleasure.

As we got closer to the back door, she released me and stumbled toward it. I followed her slowly watching, knowing she couldn't get inside without my key. She yanked on the door knob for a few seconds. With her hands on her hips she turned to me.

"Are you going to open the door or what?"

Her tone only managed to annoy me further. She tried to keep it together but the drugs were stripping the control she had over her senses.

I decided I wasn't going to wait any longer. I approached and grabbed her. With my hand on her upper arms, I pushed her against the brick wall of the building. I pressed my body against hers. I hardened at the feel of her sex against mine.

"Get off me," she said.

I laughed.

"No," I simply said.

I had no intentions of letting her go and I knew there was nothing she could do about it. The power I yielded at that moment only fueled my desire. I let my hand come up to her neck. I caressed her there. She groaned. I smiled. I knew no matter what she said, she wanted this. She wanted me to have her, to control her.

I continued my exploration of her body letting my hand slide up her thighs. I learned she wasn't wearing any panties. I reached the warmth between her thighs and again she moaned.

"No. No no no no…"

I ignored her.

As I stroked her with my fingers, she squirmed against me. Suddenly, with what little strength she had left, she pushed me. I stepped back right into a pothole. I fell backward and landed on my ass.

"Fuck!" I exclaimed.

As I climbed to my feet, my anger rose. How dare she tell me no? I was so sick of women telling me that. I knew…April would be the last.

I watched as she leaned against the wall rubbing her hands against her eyes.

"What the fuck is wrong with me?" she asked to no one in particular.

"The Xanax is kicking in…" I replied as I moved toward her.

She shook her head.

"Oh and the sleeping pills are taking effect as well…"

Her eyes grew wide.

"I…I don't…I don't take any…of…those," she slurred.

"Oh you did tonight. Next time you should stay away from other people's drinks…"

She tried to take a step forward but fell back against the wall. I took my time walking to her savoring the smell of fear in the air.

"You drugged me…with Kim's drink?"

I chuckled.

"Yes. It would have been Kim, but you just keep getting in my way."

"Leave …leave Kim alone," she said sliding down the wall until she fell on the ground.

"Once you're gone, there will be no one else to stop me," I said.

Her eyes grew wide again and in an instant…she was on the move. She crawled in the direction of the backdoor.

"Help!" she screamed.

Her yell made my heart pound in my chest. She needed to be silenced. From the ground, she began to pound on the door pleading for someone to come and help.

I knew there were people inside. Not very many but enough that she might be heard. I glanced around the alley looking for something to help silence her. I saw a large rock on the ground next to the dumpster. I grabbed the heavy object and approached.

She continued to yell. I raised the rock with both hands. I smashed it against her head. Startled, she fell and reached for the spot where the object made contact. When her hands came away they were covered in blood.

I threw the rock down and heard the thud and a splash as it fell in a puddle. She tried to crawl away down the alley toward the dumpster. I glared at her as I pulled my belt from the loops on my pants. I grabbed her feet and drug her back to me.

I straddled her body.

My weight on her back held her down as I wrapped my belt around her neck. Her hands came up blocking the black leather from wrapping around completely. I yanked her hands away and began to tighten it.

There was so much fight in her. She bucked and kicked underneath me. It felt like I was riding a bucking bull. I closed my eyes as I strangled her. My mind went back to the ecstasy I felt when I wrapped my hands around Sarah's neck and watched the life drain from her face. I thought to the night I pressed my forearm around Wendy's neck until she was limp in my arms. The pleasure was more than I had ever felt in my life.

As I continued to tighten the leather belt, I imagined penetrating her body. It had been a while since I came. I needed to have that feeling again. My memories brought me close to coming. She continued to squirm and I grinded my body against hers. She clawed at the ground and the belt hoping to free herself. I continued to slide against her, ready to explode. I heard the noises she made as she struggled to breathe. My mind turned those into sensuous groans. I hardened more than ever before. I knew that if April could make me feel this way, Kim would be extraordinary.

It took April an extended amount of time to die. It already takes several minutes to choke someone out, but she was hanging on longer than I had anticipated. My breathing was labored, but I held on. Finally she went limp and I let go. I checked her pulse.

Shit!

She was still alive. Her pulse was weak but she was still here. I was hard and ready for release. I needed something to take me over the edge. I was ready to come. I looked over and spotted the large rock again. I climbed off her and went to pick it up. I climbed back on top of her and raised the heavy object as high as I could. I smashed it against the back of her head. Again and again I hit her feeling myself get closer but…nothing. I couldn't come! Finally, I dropped the rock and fell backward completely out of breath.

I sat that way for a few minutes. Until I regained my composure. I leaned over and felt for a pulse.

It wasn't there.

I sighed.

Still breathing heavily, I stood leaving the belt around her neck. I was covered in blood and my hard-on was subsiding. I was so close! That made me hungry for more. I wanted what it seemed I couldn't have. I knew that there was only one person who would get me there.

I just needed to make a call…

CHAPTER 37

Malcolm

I had serious reservations about following Kenneth. We no longer heard pounding on the door. The screams seemed to subside. However, he insisted we still check things out.

As if on cue, the universe gave me another reason to call off this mission. A loud crack of thunder pierced the silence and suddenly we were surrounded by darkness. I stopped moving and began to plead with my brother.

"Ken, we need to just go to our cars and get out of here."

He didn't reply, yet I could hear him still moving down the hall, opening doors, checking each office. It was dark. I could barely make out his frame, but I could hear his steps as his shoes made contact with the tiled floor.

I don't know why I said anything to him at all. He wouldn't listen. I had no control over him. I rubbed my aching jaw where he hit me and realized no matter what I said, I wasn't going to get him away from Kim or any other women in this lounge.

I sighed.

Through the sounds of his footsteps, I could tell he was rushing down the hall toward the back door determined to find the source of the noise we heard. I didn't understand how he could move so fast in this darkness. It was pitch black and I had to hold onto the wall, using touch in place of sight.

Not like I was in a hurry, however. My first instinct was to call the police. We didn't need to be out there on our own trying to save someone. There were people paid to do that. Yet calling the police would only add to the problems here. If there wasn't anyone in trouble out there it would just be another reason for the police to snoop around and possibly find something incriminating.

As much as I hated to admit it, he was right. We needed to see what was going on.

"Ken, stop," I said.

To my surprise he did.

"Malcolm, we need to see if someone is hurt," he replied.

"I know, but we need a plan. We can't just barge out there..."

"The longer we wait and talk about formulating a plan, a woman could be dead."

He continued his journey down the long dark hallway not waiting on a response from me. I had no choice but to follow. I couldn't let him go out there by himself. I walked cautiously while my brother barreled down the hall determined to be some woman's super hero.

As we passed the video control room, it was then that I remembered Tony. He had been watching and hiding video tapes when I left him.

"Ken, wait," I said.

I took a couple of steps into the room. I couldn't see a damn thing.

"Tony! Tony!" I yelled.

No answer. That shocked me, but then I had a thought.

"Hey maybe that was Tony banging on the back door. He may have gone out for a smoke and left his keys."

That made more sense than anything I could think of. There were no women in the lounge tonight so how could there be a woman in danger?

"What about the scream?" Kenneth asked. "That didn't sound like a man screaming?"

He had a point, but what woman would be in the alley this late at night. Then I thought about Sasha. She hadn't been gone very long. What if she was snatched up by the killer and that was her screaming? My worry began to match Kenneth's.

"Well, I guess there is only one way to find out. Open the door," I replied.

He did as I said.

The smell of rain and rancid food from the dumpster hit me as we exited the building. Kenneth ran out into the darkness without a care. I waited holding open the door. I knew that once you exited this door there was no return without a key. I looked around for something to prop the door open. Sasha locked the front door and our only way back inside needed a large object to keep it ajar.

"Kenneth," I said looking around. "It's too dark out here to see or help anyone."

Although the alley was more illuminated than the inside of the building, there was only one street light on the corner that added some light. But...not very much. It was still hard to see and that made this mission pretty dangerous. Kenneth didn't have a clue what happened in this alley just a week and a half ago. He didn't see what I saw on the video footage. Tony and I watched a psychopath drag Ashley down the alley to her death.

The police told me she was found butchered and it affected me that I possibly had footage...well at least Tony had footage of her assailant. My gut was telling me we needed to get out of this alley and we needed to do it NOW!

"Ken, c'mon. I don't see anyone or anything for that matter," I said taking a few steps into the abyss but making sure I kept a hold of the door. "You're not going to be someone's knight in shining armor tonight."

He ignored me and began to walk down the alley toward the front entrance.

I sighed.

I looked around for something to hold the door, when I spotted a large rock sitting in a puddle. I reached over leaving my foot to hold the door open and grabbed it. It was heavy, wet and...sticky.

I sat the rock against the door. The weight was perfect to keep it open.

I took a few steps away from the back entrance wiping my hands on my pants. By this time, Kenneth had pulled out his cell phone in order to illuminate the alley. He walked back toward me then past me in the direction of the dumpster. I could only make out the light from his phone and his shirt. I heard his large feet sloshing in the puddles.

Man! He was relentless. He wasn't going to give up until he checked the entire alley. I went from worried to annoyed in a hurry.

"Kenneth!" I yelled. "Let's..."

"Malcolm!" he called back.

I immediately stopped talking. At that moment thunder roared and I looked up at the sky expecting the second coming of Jesus.

My heart began to race. The hairs on the back of my neck stood on end. I could tell by Kenneth's tone...something was wrong.

"Kenneth, what's going on?" I questioned.

God! I hope he didn't find another dead body. This lounge would never reopen if that was the case. Plus my brother would never get over seeing something like that. I moved a little closer. The light on his phone had gone out and the only thing I could see was the back of his white shirt.

"Malcolm" he finally said. "Just stay there."

I knew at that moment we had lost another girl. The only person I could think of was Sasha.

I sighed.

That's when I heard another voice in the distance.

"Are you fucking crazy?" Kenneth responded.

I had no clue what the other person said. They were speaking in hushed tones.

"I'm not leaving until you let her go," Kenneth replied.

Let who go?

"Ken, who the hell are you talking to?" I asked.

I couldn't see anyone and I was starting to wonder if my brother had lost his mind.

"Malcolm, just listen to me. Stay there."

Then I heard him say, "You don't want to do that."

I went into big brother protect mode. I took a step forward only to be met by these words.

"Listen to your brother Malcolm and stay there."

I recognized that voice. Yet it was different. There was a sinister tilt to the tone that put me on edge. I didn't intend to leave my brother at the end of a dark alley without me. I moved forward quickly ignoring their direction.

That is when it happened.

My foot hit a mound of trash or something that caused me to lose my balance. I spilled forward onto the ground. Pain radiated throughout my body from my shoulder that broke my fall.

It took me a minute to recover as I tried to move quickly to my feet. I put my hand down trying to maneuver off the concrete when it landed on another hand...one that didn't belong to me. I freaked out. I jerked my hand back and squinted. I realized then that the mound was much more than that.

I pulled my cell from my pocket and with shaking fingers I manage to turn on the flashlight feature. I slowly moved it to the person on the ground. I was expecting to see Sasha but was shocked when I came face to face with...April.

Her eyes were closed and blood ran down her face. I moved the light and saw her hair was matted with more blood. I slowly reached over and checked her neck for a pulse. There was none. She was gone.

My body began to shake and I could feel vomit rising to the surface. I scrambled backward and rose to my feet.

"Ken, she's dead." I managed to tell him.

I flashed my light his way and noticed his arms were up as in surrender. Before I had a chance to react, I watched as my brother lunged forward. It was then that I heard a loud pop.

I ran forward just as I saw my brother hit the ground.

CHAPTER 38

Kimberly

I tasted the saltiness of his sweaty hands. He continued to cover my mouth and my nose. I could barely breathe. The sweat was mixed with another flavor. I knew in my gut it was blood.

I had to throw up.

Was it April's blood?

I began to struggle in his arms. Despite the gun in my back, I was going to be sick and I needed him to let me go. I moaned, as it was all I could do.

"What is wrong with you?" he asked.

I tried to tell him that I was going to choke on my own vomit.

"What are you trying to say?"

How could I tell him with his hand over my mouth? I continued to whimper and make noises. He pressed the gun harder into the small of my back. I went silent.

"I'm going to move my hand," he began leaning in close. "If you scream, I'm going to kill you."

Slowly he moved his hand. It was just in time. I felt pain in my stomach and burps that tasted like acid from my stomach rose to the surface. Once his hand was moved, I blurted out.

"I'm going to be sick…"

He let me go and I moved toward the fence. The instant I bent over, I released my dinner all over the ground. I wiped my mouth with the sleeve of my hoodie trying to remove the blood, sweat and barf from my lips.

"Are you okay?" he asked.

"Do you care?" I managed to say waiting on the next round of throw up to arrive.

He sighed.

"Of course I care. I wouldn't be here if I didn't."

Was he serious? Did he really think holding me against my will and attacking April was showing he cared?

My mind went to April and I looked over at her. I could barely make out her frame near the dumpster.

"What did you do to April?" I questioned. "We need to get her help."

He continued to point the gun at me.

"April is beyond help," he responded. "She put herself in that situation. Now she can no longer get in my way."

I threw up again.

My worst nightmare had come true. April was dead. I knew that if she continued to see clients bad things would happen. I warned her repeatedly. I thought it would be the strangers that would get her. I had no clue that she would fall victim to someone she trusted. I was heartbroken. I dropped to my knees and cried.

"Calm down," he said taking a step toward me. He reached down and placed his hand on my shoulder. I shook it off. I didn't want him to touch me. Never again.

That only seemed to anger him.

"Get up!" he ordered.

I didn't move.

I closed my eyes and tried to calm myself. I knew there was no time to grieve right now. He could be lying to me. April could just need help and I needed to get it for her. I had to get away from him. As I was on my knees, I spotted an old 2x4 lying against the fence that separated the lounge and the alley from the building next to it. I tried to bypass the vomit and reach for it. Before I had the chance, I felt the gun pressed against the back of my head.

"Don't think about it. Do you want a bullet in your brain?"

I shook my head.

"Why are you doing this?" I asked. I started to cry again.

"I don't want it to be this way. Just get up and follow me to my car. We can just get away from here. I know that's what you want. Then you and I can be together."

"What if I don't want to be with you?"

"Do you think you have a choice?" he asked.

"Did you really kill April?" I questioned.

"Yes," he replied with no emotion.

"You're a monster!"

He grunted like a wild animal before he spoke.

"I'm no monster," he said through gritted teeth.

Then he moved the gun away from my head. I turned to look at him.

Lightning flashed across the sky and lit up the alley for a second. It was then I noticed the amount of blood all over his clothes. I felt as if I was going to throw up again.

"I did this all for you. I am no monster."

What did he do for me?

"You killed April for me?"

He laughed. It was a sinister laugh. One that sent chills down my spine.

"Not just April. I made quick work of Wendy just for you. I made sure she could never hurt you again."

My eyes widened at his words. I began to shake. I felt weak. I struggled to breathe. He killed Wendy? I didn't know what to believe. Was he telling me this to scare me? I looked over at April and realized he was telling the truth. There was too much blood. And if he killed April...he must have killed Wendy.

Then I thought of Ashley.

"Did you kill Ashley too? Was that for me?"

He opened his mouth to speak but was interrupted by sounds coming from the back door.

"Get up!" he said.

"No," I said refusing to move.

He pushed the pistol in my back between my shoulder blades.

"GET. UP!"

He reached down and grabbed me. I wanted to fight him but I knew that attacking someone with a gun wasn't a bright idea. I climbed to my feet and he pulled me against him into the darkness.

A roll of thunder roared through the city just as the back door opened. Out walked Kenneth and Malcolm.

My captor held me closely against his body. His warm breath on my ear reminded me of the danger I was in.

"Say a word," he whispered. "and you're dead."

He moved the gun from my back and pointed it at my temple.

I watched silently and fearfully as Kenneth walked away from me down the opposite end of the alley. Malcolm stayed close to the door.

"Kenneth," Malcolm said. "It's too dark out here to see or help anyone."

He seemed reluctant to venture out into the night. I didn't blame him. I wished I had just left the club and gone home like my gut was telling me to. I wanted to risk it and make some kind of noise. I wanted Kenneth or Malcolm to save me but fear of dying kept me silent.

Where we were standing it was too dark for them to see us. The shadows hid us in its folds. I wanted Kenneth to find me but I also didn't want him to get hurt in the process.

"Ken, c'mon. I don't see anyone or anything for that matter," Malcolm said.

Kenneth ignored him and pulled out his phone. He used it as a flashlight so he could see better. He made it to one end of the alley then turned and headed back toward the back door where Malcolm was standing. My heart sank. I didn't want to be left alone again with this psycho. I began to shake and whimper.

"Quiet," he whispered.

I could feel my captor's heart beating. He was worried. I knew he didn't want the Johnson brothers to find us. Kenneth didn't help him any. It seemed like he was looking for something and he wasn't going to stop until he found it.

I watched as he turned toward us. He froze for a second and raised his phone again. Instead of going back inside, Kenneth came our way. He walked close to the dumpster where we were standing. In an attempt to keep us unseen, my abductor practically drug me backward down the alley and placed one hand over my mouth.

Kenneth squinted his eyes.

The gun was still pointed at my head.

I heard what sounded like a gasp escape from Kenneth's mouth. I knew he saw us. He lowered his phone.

"What the hell is going on here?" he asked.

"It's none of your business. Just back up and go back inside."

"I heard a scream. Kim, are you okay?" Kenneth asked softly.

I vigorously shook my head. I was fully aware he had yet to see the gun or he wouldn't be so calm. It was also why he took a few steps closer. That is when the weapon left my head and was pointed directly at Kenneth.

"I said back up and go inside. This has nothing to do with you or Malcolm."

"Kenneth!" Malcolm called. "Let's…"

"Malcolm!" Kenneth called back.

He kept his eyes on the gun. He made eye contact with me and I tried to portray all the fear and terror I felt. He must have understood because he nodded.

"Kenneth, what's going on?" Malcolm asked.

No matter what, Malcolm stayed close to the door. He refused to enter into the void like Kenneth. I had no idea if that made him smart or a wimp.

"Malcolm" Kenneth pleaded with him. "Just stay there."

"Kenneth, walk away. Or I'm," he took the gun and pointed it at my head again. "I'm going to kill her."

Kenneth raised his hands.

"Are you fucking crazy?"

My captor laughed.

"I may be crazy. However, you can't have her, she's mine. And I will do anything to keep Kim. Even if that means no one has her. I would rather she be dead than for you or Malcolm to take her from me."

He spoke as if I wasn't there. Tears poured hotly down my cheeks. This man was serious. He would kill me and not feel any remorse. I knew I didn't want to die. I began to make more noises. I wanted Kenneth to know he was serious. He's killed before and would kill me if pushed.

I moved my eyes in the direction of April's body. I knew it was dark but I had no clue how they hadn't seen her.

Kenneth didn't pick up on my hints. He had no idea he was dealing with a murderer.

"So, go back inside, or better yet, get in your car and leave. Take your brother with you. I am sick of you two. You think you can just abuse and take advantage of these girls. I free them from this life."

My eyes grew large.

"I'm not leaving until you let her go," Kenneth replied.

"Ken, who the hell are you talking to?" I heard from the back door.

"Malcolm, just listen to me. Stay there."

Kenneth took a step toward us. I was pulled backward with a hand still over my mouth and a gun pointed at me. Kenneth moved forward again and we moved back even further. Finally he pulled the gun away from me and aimed it at Kenneth. This time I heard something click on the gun and I knew he would shoot Kenneth if he had the chance.

"You don't want to do that," Kenneth said.

On the corner of my eye I saw movement. I guess Malcolm finally realized something wasn't right and he took a step toward us. My abductor noticed.

"Listen to your brother Malcolm and stay there."

My eyes went back to Kenneth. I wanted him to save me but I also wanted him to leave before he was hurt. Even though I broke up with him I knew deep down my feelings were still strong. The last thing I wanted was for something bad to happen to him because of me.

"Ken, she's dead." I heard Malcolm call out.

Kenneth turned and looked over to where Malcolm was standing. It was then that he finally noticed the woman on the ground.

I began to cry again. It was confirmed. April was gone.

Then his eyes met mine. I wondered if he could see the fear in them.

Kenneth's eyes went back to April and his brother and then back to me. I was convinced he now understood the danger we all were in. This man holding a gun on me was dangerous and willing to kill.

I heard Kenneth take a deep breath then let it out.

Then without warning, he lunged at us.

It was quick.

It was deliberate.

It wasn't enough.

I screamed as the loud noise pierced the night air.

CHAPTER 39

Kenneth

The impact and hot searing pain dropped me to the ground. It was overpowering. My left shoulder burned with an intensity I had never felt before. I had no clue what happened. I was in shock. I laid flat on the wet, cold ground trying to comprehend the predicament I was in.

The noise all around me was muted and swallowed up by the ringing in my ears. I could barely hear someone screaming and a deep voice yelling. Are they calling my name?

Finally, I touched the ache in my shoulder. I pulled my hand back and brought it to my face. My fingers were red and sticky. Suddenly I felt my body being grabbed. That only added to my pain. I grunted.

"We have to get something on this wound." I heard Malcolm say.

I turned my head and watched in a daze as he undid his neck tie.

"Shit!" I yelled as he pressed it into the gash.

"You're going to be okay, Ken," Malcolm said as he wrapped the tie around my shoulder and arm. "It looks like the bullet went straight through."

"That doesn't make me feel any better," I said through gritted teeth as he tied it off.

I grimaced as he patted my left shoulder. I could feel myself begin to sweat and I felt nauseous from the pain.

"It could have been worse," he said in a low voice.

He didn't sound too happy with me. I could understand. Lunging at a man with a gun may not have been the best idea.

"I had to save Kim," I said breathless struggling to manage my discomfort.

"You can't save Kim if you're dead."

He had a point.

Malcolm turned his attention from me to the killer. He still had the pistol pointed in our direction.

"You shot my brother. What the fuck is wrong with you?"

I leaned on my right side and used that as leverage to sit up. The gun was shaking in his hand and I realized how lucky I was.

"I didn't want to do that…" he replied.

He held his hand over Kim's mouth. Her eyes were closed as if she were sleeping or praying.

"You should have just listened to me and backed off," he said locking eyes with me. "I didn't want to shoot you."

"Just let Kim go and we can all just walk away from this. None of us will say anything about April," Malcolm said standing with his hands up.

I looked up at my brother.

"What are you talking about Mal? What happened to April?"

He looked down at me and sighed.

"April's dead!"

He pointed toward the back door. There wasn't much light but I could see a mound of something between the backdoor and the dumpster. My head whipped back toward the man holding Kim.

"He killed April?" I asked.

"I don't think he only killed April..." my brother responded.

I looked over at Malcolm with my eyes enlarged. He stared at me and I saw something I rarely see. Fear? My brother was afraid. He was scared of the man standing before us with the gun now pointed at Kim's temple. I thought about the other women. Sarah, Abigail, Wendy, Ashley and now April. They didn't deserve to die the way they did.

I was instantly as terrified as my brother. Not for myself. But for Kim. We had a serial killer in our midst and he had his arms around her.

It made perfect sense. He had access to all the girls. He was someone they all trusted. It made me sick to my stomach. To think he took advantage of that to end their lives...

"You're a monster!" I yelled trying to get to my feet.

"I AM NOT A MONSTER!" he yelled back.

He pointed the gun at me.

"But now you know I'm serious. I will shoot you both if you don't back off and leave Kim and me alone."

"Never!" I said through clenched teeth.

I had managed to stand despite the pain radiating throughout my left arm. By this point it felt as though it had been beaten repeatedly with a bat.

"Okay, okay, okay," Malcolm said hands out standing between me and the gunman. "Let's all calm down."

At that moment the sky opened up and it began to rain again. Not as fiercely as before but steady small drops pelted us. The raindrops hitting the pavement and thunder in the distance were the only sounds that could be heard in the alley as we all glared at each other in silence.

After a couple of minutes, Malcolm spoke.

"Now, let's see if we can all talk this out."

"There is nothing to talk about. He just needs to let Kim go before I beat his ass." I said.

"Try it and next time I'll make sure I hit a vital organ."

Kim began to whimper and squirm in his arms. He pulled her tighter and brought the gun back to her. My anger was surpassing levels it had never reached before.

"Look, guys. Let's not threaten each other. We're all friends…" Malcolm began.

"Friends? We are not friends. Neither of you give a damn about me. Kim is the only one here that cares. Right Kim?"

My eyes locked with hers just as they widened. She pleaded with me for direction. She needed me to tell her how to respond. I nodded. We had to do what we had to do to keep her safe. She mimicked me and nodded also.

"We've known each other for years. Do you really need a gun?" Malcolm asked taking a step closer. The gunman took a step back dragging Kim against him in the process.

"Put the gun down and we can all chat about this."

"No!" he said with the weapon shaking in his hand. He must have been scared shitless. If he didn't have that pistol, he wouldn't have been so quick with the threats.

"He won't put it down. He's a pussy." I blurted.

"Ken, shut up!" Malcolm said glaring at me. Then he whispered. "I'm trying to negotiate here."

I took a deep breath trying to swallow my fear and anger. I tried hard to keep my mouth shut.

"There is no negotiating," the gunman said. "Kim and I are leaving and you two better walk away and let us go or I will kill everyone here."

"Why do you need Kim so bad? Just let her go with us and you can disappear. We won't call the police. We won't say a word." Malcolm pleaded with him.

He shook his head.

Then he began to laugh.

It was a loud sinister laugh and was made creepier by the roar of thunder that came at that moment. I shuddered.

"You don't get it. Kim is special to me. I need her. The first time I laid eyes on her, touched her, kissed her...I knew she was mine," he said.

He was crazy. He had to be. Killers are never in their right mind. How could we trust him to let Kim go? He could shoot us for knowing the truth and do what he wanted with Kim. That made this situation much more dangerous.

He began to mumble to himself while backing down the alley. Kim refused to go. He had to practically drag her. She fought and screamed but he held her firmly with the gun trained on us.

"Where are you going?" I asked him.

He didn't answer. He continued to drag her backwards.

"If you care about Kim, you will let her go. Look how frightened she is. You just killed her best friend and shot her..." Malcolm paused. He looked over at me then back at the killer. "You just shot someone in front of her. If you truly loved her, you would let her go."

"It's because I love her that she needs to be with me. I can take care of her and she can take care of me."

"Then why do you have a gun pointed at her head?" I asked taking a large step forward.

It must have made him uncomfortable because he pointed the gun squarely at me.

"Back up!"

Malcolm turned to look at me and shook his head. I knew he didn't want to see me shot again. It could be worse if he took aim this time. I was still in a lot of pain so the thought of being shot again made me back off. Yet I knew I couldn't just let him take Kim off somewhere without putting up a fight.

"Okay, you can have her." Malcolm said to the surprise of everyone.

All eyes were on him.

"What?" I questioned.

"Ken just be quiet."

I looked him in the eyes and saw something. It was no longer fear. I saw determination and a resolve to put an end to this.

He brought his attention back to the killer.

"Take Kim. Since you love her so much I know you won't hurt her. Just don't hurt my brother."

Kim continued to struggle in his arms. I could tell she believed Malcolm would just leave her with him. She was fighting and I knew that if she could, I would have no problem fighting for her.

Then the killer smiled. *The motherfucker had the audacity to smile!*

My anger was threatening to boil over. I knew that my brother wouldn't just leave her. I could tell that Malcolm had a plan but I didn't know how much longer I could take it especially since that bastard began to drag her further down the alley.

"You can't do that!" I said moving closer to him and Kim. To my surprise, Malcolm moved closer as well.

"I can do whatever I want. I have the gun."

I looked at my brother trying to figure out what his next step would be. I knew him well enough to know he hadn't learned from my mistake. This killer may have the gun now, but Malcolm was done negotiating.

CHAPTER 40

She completes you. You have to get away. You have to get Kim out of here.

Those thoughts ran through my head. The solid piece of steel felt hot in my hands. Kim's warm body suddenly went stiff as the loud noise of the gun stole the silence from the night.

I watched in fear and disbelief as Kenneth hit the ground. Kim pressed her body against mine and my focus was no longer on the bullet I released but on how good she made me feel.

"You shot my brother. What the fuck is wrong with you?" Malcolm asked.

They didn't understand. I didn't have time to think. Time to process what my next step would be. He gave me no choice. You never come at someone holding a gun...

"I didn't want to do that..." I replied. "You should have just listened to me and backed off," I held the gun pointed at Kim's head. "I didn't want to shoot you."

"Just let Kim go and we can all just walk away from this. None of us will say anything about April," Malcolm said standing with his hands up.

I didn't trust him. I knew that if his brother could attack me...he would too.

She completes you. You have to go. You have to get Kim out of here.

I shook my head trying to get away from my thoughts. I knew what I had to do. There was only one life I needed to take. Yet if I had to...I would clear out this entire alley.

"What are you talking about Mal? What happened to April?" Kenneth asked.

"April is dead."

Thinking about April brought back memories of watching the life dissipate from her body. With every pull of the belt I felt myself getting closer and closer...

"He killed April?"

"I don't think he only killed April..." Malcolm replied.

They both glared at me. I felt exposed. They knew all my secrets. How could I let any of them walk away now? They would never understand my sacrifice. I actually liked April. But like Kenneth and Malcolm, she got in my way.

"You're a monster!" Kenneth yelled.

He fought to stand holding the tie wrapped around his arm.

"I AM NOT A MONSTER!" I yelled back.

I was offended. I was not a monster...or crazy. Kim called me a monster too. That only fueled my anger. Obsessed...maybe. Was I obsessed with Kim? NO. I was obsessed with what Kim could do for me. That was why I had to keep her away from the Johnson brothers. They wanted to use her. I wanted to sacrifice her. Give her the chance to be more than an escort. She would be my martyr. She would die for a cause.

I pointed the gun at him.

"But now you know I'm serious. I will shoot you both if you don't back off and leave Kim and me alone."

"Never!" Kenneth said making a move toward me.

I knew that I would shoot him again if I had to. I didn't want to but I knew I would do anything to keep Kim with me. I didn't want to kill him. I sacrificed the women for a higher purpose. But to murder just to do so…that wasn't my goal.

Plans can change.

"Okay, okay, okay," Malcolm said hands up standing between me and Kenneth. "Let's all calm down."

We were silent. Even Kim stopped squirming in my arms. All attention was on Malcolm.

When everyone seemed to have calmed down, Malcolm spoke.

"Now, let's see if we can all talk this out."

"There is nothing to talk about. He just needs to let Kim go before I beat his ass." Kenneth said.

It seemed he hadn't learned anything from the hole in his shoulder. I cocked my head to the side with the gun still pointed at him.

"Try it and next time I'll make sure I hit a vital organ," I warned.

Kim began to whimper and squirm. I pulled her tighter and brought the gun back to her temple. She continued to move and wiggle in my arms. The motion turned me on and I could feel myself harden. Although I was slightly losing my grip on her, I was reluctant to make her stop.

"Look, guys. Let's not threaten each other. We're all friends…" Malcolm began.

His words surprised me. I eyed him suspiciously.

"Friends? We are not friends. Neither of you give a damn about me. Kim is the only one here that cares. Right Kim?"

She nodded.

I knew she cared about me as much as I cared about her. I've known the Johnson brothers for years. They were selfish, self-centered and only in this life for themselves. They didn't care about me or Kim. It's because I loved Kim I knew she would be the one to bring me back from the dead. Make me whole again. I didn't care about the other women. I believed that was the problem. It was why I couldn't come inside of them.

"We've known each other for years. Do you really need a gun?" Malcolm asked taking a step closer.

She completes you. You have to get away. You have to get Kim out of here.

I took a step back.

"Put the gun down and we can all chat about this."

"No!" I said.

I was livid, afraid and turned on all at the same time. The hand with the gun shook.

"He won't put it down. He's a pussy." Kenneth yelled.

"Ken, shut up!" Malcolm said. "I'm trying to negotiate here."

They were talking about me like I wasn't standing here. It was the way everyone treated me. I lived my life as the invisible man and only reappeared when others needed something. Wanted something from me.

The heat from my anger burned me from the inside out.

"There is no negotiating," I said. "Kim and I are leaving and you two better walk away and let us go or I will kill everyone here."

"Why do you need Kim so bad? Just let her go with us and you can disappear. We won't call the police. We won't say a word." Malcolm begged.

That wasn't going to work. Did they really think I was stupid? I knew when and if they walked away they would tell the police exactly what took place here. They would also inform them that I was the one that killed the women. They would tell everyone that would listen. I understood I was going down for this. But, if I was going down I was taking Kim with me.

Then I began to laugh.

It was a loud and crazy sounding. Even to me. It was timed perfectly with the roaring thunder in the background. Even in the dark I could make out the look of confusion on the guys faces.

It was almost comical how far I would go to orgasm. It warped my mind and I had no clue what was up and what was down. Yet, I knew it was much more than an orgasm that fueled me. I wanted to be seen. I wanted women to see me as an equal. The women in this club and in other parts of my life saw me as someone they could push around. I was going to demand their respect. If they wouldn't respect me…then they deserved to be the next to forfeit their life.

The brothers didn't understand what Kim meant to me.

She completes me.

They had plenty of women that could make them feel special and make them come all night long. I didn't. I hadn't had that in years. I was desperate. I came so close when I took April's life. She brought me close but oh so short of the goal.

"You don't get it. Kim is special to me. I need her. The first time I laid eyes on her, touched her, kissed her…I knew she was mine," I confessed.

She completes you. You have to go. You have to get Kim out of here.

Quietly I began to speak to Kim.

"It's okay. I will make sure you go quickly. I love you. I will make sure you go quickly. Not like the others…"

She whimpered and moaned at hearing my words.

I began to move backwards trying to protect her. I had to get her to my apartment. The one nobody knew about. The one that held all my drugs...

Kim refused to go. It was if her feet were stuck in cement. They wouldn't move. I began to drag her down the alley.

"Please don't make me kill you right here," I whispered to her.

She still refused to move.

"Where are you going?" Kenneth asked me.

I couldn't tell him. No one knew about my secret place not far from here.

"If you care about Kim, you will let her go," Malcolm said attempting to trick me with his words. "Look how frightened she is. You just killed her best friend and shot her…" Malcolm paused. "You just shot someone in front of her. If you truly loved her, you would let her go."

"It's because I love her that she needs to be with me," I responded. "I can take care of her and she can take care of me."

"Then why do you have a gun pointed at her head?" Kenneth asked taking a large step forward.

I moved the gun away from Kim and pointed it at Kenneth. I knew what he was capable of. He had already tried to jump me once. He was a determined bastard. He may try something again.

"Back up!" I yelled.

Malcolm took a step forward as well. I took a step back squeezing Kim's body against mine. They wanted her. They wanted to take her away from me. I wouldn't let them. I had waited long enough for this moment and I was going to have it.

"Okay, you can have her." Malcolm said.

I glared at him. I was suspicious. I took another step back again bringing Kim with me.

"What?" Kenneth said.

"Ken just be quiet."

Though I was shocked he said it, I wasn't surprised. I knew Malcolm valued his life and his brother's life over Kim's. It didn't matter what he said, however. They should have watched enough crime TV to know that I couldn't just let them leave here. I had to kill them. It was decided for me the moment they realized I killed the women. It would pain me to do it but they had to go.

"Take Kim. Since you love her so much I know you won't hurt her. Just don't hurt my brother."

Kim began to struggle in my arms again. This time much more vigorously. It was difficult to hold onto her while she thrashed about. It seemed she finally realized they didn't care about her. This entire time she was in denial about her fate. Now that she knew the truth about the Johnson brothers, she tried to battle for her life. It increased my desire for her even more. I was turned on by the fight in her and knew once the life drained from her body I would have felt the most pleasure I had felt in a very long time.

I smiled just thinking about it.

I became impatient and I began to drag her further down the alley. I needed to get her away before she no longer wanted to fight.

"You can't do that!" Kenneth said.

Both brothers moved closer.

It made me more determined to kill them.

"I can do whatever I want. I have the gun," I reminded them.

They both took another step toward me.

You have to kill them...NOW!

I took the gun and pointed it at the two men in front of me.

Foolishly I let my focus stay on the brothers just a minute too long. What made Kim so attractive to me became my downfall. Her flailing about turned ferocious and I, for a second, lost my grip on her.

That was when she punched me.

In the balls.

The pain was fierce and came on strong. It wasn't just a localized pain. It ran up my body into my abdomen. I felt as if I were going to vomit. I managed to hold onto the gun but I was in so much pain I couldn't use it. I didn't have much time to recuperate before I felt something like a battering ram hit me.

That was when the gun went off for the second time.

CHAPTER 41

Malcolm

"What?" Kenneth said.

The alley was silent except for the thunder in the distance. Everyone seemed to be in shock by my words.

I surprised myself when the words exited my mouth. Once they were out there, I had to roll with them.

I turned to my brother and held up my hand.

"Ken just be quiet."

I brought my attention back to the man holding Kim hostage and lied to him.

"Take Kim. Since you love her so much I know you won't hurt her. Just don't hurt my brother."

I had no intentions of just walking away, however. No. I wouldn't leave Kim alone with this psychotic motherfucker. I just needed a moment to plan. To throw him off. And it seemed like my spur of the moment strategy was working. His eyes were narrowed and his focus was on me…and not Kim.

As if on cue, she began to struggle in his arms. She wiggled and flailed. Despite having a gun pointed at her, she was determined to not let him take her.

I had enough cop friends to know…you do not let a captor take you to a second location. It was less likely you would survive. Kim must have been versed in this because she threw her shoulder into him and twisted trying to free herself. He reacted by pulling her further down the alley dragging her with his hand over her mouth.

"You can't do that!" Kenneth yelled at him taking a step closer. I followed suit knowing that if he left here with Kim she was probably going to end up like April. I couldn't have that on my conscience.

"I can do whatever I want. I have the gun," he said.

It wasn't lost on me that he had a gun pointed directly at us. My goal was to figure out a way to get it from him. I just didn't know how I was going to do that without someone being killed.

I took another step forward. I stopped when he pointed the gun directly at me then at Kenneth then at me again. His hand continued to shake. My eyes went from the pistol…to Kim. She was screaming. It was muffled by his hand but she was screaming and struggling.

Fighting for her life.

My mind was set on getting the firearm. I moved another step forward. The gun swung in my direction. My heart was pounding out of my chest. I could hear the blood rushing throughout my body. I was on high alert and…I was afraid.

I was terrified of my next move.

While I was trying to come to terms with what I had to do, Kim was making moves of her own. It seemed as if she didn't care he had a gun. She fought and wiggled. She wrestled and squirmed.

The rest seemed to happen in slow motion.

He had no idea who to focus on. He mistakenly decided that my brother and I were the bigger threat. He kept the gun trained on us as he tried to reestablish control over Kim. It didn't work. She was able to slide a centimeter to the left side. That was all the space she needed. Bravely, with her right hand, she punched him.

Squarely in the balls.

Being a man, I knew exactly how painful it had to be. My own scrotum clinched and tingled in response. He immediately released her and grabbed for his crotch. I could feel his pain, yet there was no time for sympathy.

It was time to move.

I had only a split second. Only enough time to take a breath and act!

I threw caution and common sense out the window and lunged at him head first. I apparently learned no lessons after seeing my brother being shot. I went at him like a linebacker.

As I made contact, a loud crack tore through the silence.

Did he try to shoot me? Was I shot?

It was too late for those thoughts now. If I were shot, it didn't stop my momentum as I smashed into him taking him down to the ground with me. Our bodies hit the wet pavement with a sick thud. The impact knocked the wind out of me.

When we landed, the gun flew out of his hands. I didn't notice at first. I was prepared to fight an armed man.

"Malcolm!" I heard my brother scream.

I rolled off the killer and checked my body to see if I had been shot. I seemed fine. I looked over and saw the gunman looking for his weapon. It was dark and I'm sure it was almost impossible to see where it ended up. He felt around on the ground and I saw this as my chance to get the better of him. I could take him without it.

I jumped on top of him and punched him in the face. I was angry and didn't realize how mad I was until I had him beneath me. I continued to punch him punishing him for what he did to my brother. What he did to all the women that were killed. I didn't notice that as I was punching, he was reaching for a rock. When he grabbed it, he used it to hit me in the face. I fell off him and landed in a puddle.

He climbed on top of me and used the rock hit me in the face again. He tried to hit me a third time but I grabbed his wrist with my left hand and swung landing a blow with my right against his jaw. He collapsed on the ground.

After that, the world felt as if it were being fast forwarded.

Lightening lit up the sky and the alley for just a second. That was all it took for us both to lay eyes on the gun. I didn't waste time. I scrambled on my knees trying to get to it. I was almost there when I felt someone grab my ankles and pull. I lost my balance and landed flat on my face.

"Shit!" I exclaimed.

He didn't squander. He immediately went for it.

"Kenneth, get the gun!" I yelled.

Ken, who was foolishly comforting Kim, wasn't able to move fast enough. Just as the killer reached the gun, I was on his back. I grabbed his hand and tried to pry it from him. We rolled back and forth. I would be on top of him and then we would roll and he'd end up on top of me as we wrestled.

"I'm going to kill you!" he growled.

From his look I knew he was serious. I could see the fury in eyes and his mouth was positioned into a snarl. In all the years I had known him, I'd never seen him this way. The amount of anger it seemed he had for me at that moment was chilling.

He really planned to kill me.
I didn't plan to die.

My adrenaline was pumping and I realized this situation was a matter of life and death. I had to get the gun or someone for sure was going to be killed. He was much stronger than I realized and I was struggling to get the gun from him.

We continued to wrestle when out of nowhere I was smashed across the back with a solid and hard object.

It was Kim.

It seemed she had decided she couldn't watch me fight any longer. Wielding a large piece of wood, she attempted to hit her captor with it. As we rolled around on the ground, she swung with abandon. That was how I was hit. I now had the added bonus of dodging a 2x4 as well as blows coming from below.

He pushed the gun down trying to free his wrist from my grasp. I noticed his fingers were frighteningly close to the trigger. I was now on the bottom and tried to roll where I would be on top. We ended up on our sides trying to land blows. The gun was squashed between us. I could feel the barrel against my gut.

I didn't like that position. I tried with to bring the gun back up. He fought me trying to draw back his wrist. I knew that if had gotten free he would shoot me. I couldn't let that happen. I pulled and he pulled as our bodies were locked so close together in a dangerous embrace.

Thunder roared at that moment. It was closer than ever before. The boom didn't mask the next sound. The third loud crack of the night penetrated the groaning and growling of our fight.

There was nothing but silence after that. There was a ringing in my ears from the sound of the gun.

Everyone froze. I held on to him afraid of what just happened.

When we finally rolled apart, the gun dropped to the ground with a clunk. Neither of us moved to retrieve it. I could barely make out footsteps rushing over to us. I shook my head for clarity but none was there. I was in a daze.

I felt something on my stomach.

I reached for it.

Then I brought my fingers to my face.

There was a dark substance. It was wet and sticky. My mind registered it was blood. I hated blood. I couldn't stand to see it.

Then everything went black.

CHAPTER 42

Kimberly

His words sent a shiver down my spine.

"It's okay. I will make sure you go quickly. I love you. I will make sure you go quickly. Not like the others…"

I closed my eyes and hoped this was all a dream. I would open them and April would be alive, Kenneth wouldn't be shot and a gun wouldn't be pointed at my head.

He began to pull me backwards. I refused to move. The last thing I wanted was to be alone with him again. There was at least some hope I would survive now that Malcolm and Kenneth were here. He attempted to drag me. I dug in my heels.

He wasn't letting up, however.

I could tell he was getting angry I refused to cooperate.

"Please don't make me kill you right here," he growled in my ear.

I still had no plans to go with him. If he wanted to off me he would have to do it here...in this alley.

"Where are you going?" Kenneth asked my captor. I could hear the fear in his voice.

He knew what I was aware of. If I was taken away…I wasn't coming back.

That fear almost made me vomit again.

"If you care about Kim, you will let her go," Malcolm said taking a step forward.. "Look how frightened she is. You just killed her best friend and shot her…" Malcolm said pausing. "You just shot someone in front of her. If you truly loved her, you would let her go."

"It's because I love her that she needs to be with me," he replied pressing the gun firmly against my temple. "I can take care of her and she can take care of me."

"Then why do you have a gun pointed at her head?" Kenneth asked moving forward.

He removed the gun from me and pointed it squarely at Kenneth. That worried me. The last time he had the gun pointed at Kenneth he shot him. I knew the next wound would be fatal. Kenneth already looked terrible. Every few minutes he grimaced from the pain. It was dark but he was close enough that I could see Malcolm's tie was not stopping the blood from oozing from his body.

"Back up!" the gunman yelled.

Malcolm moved forward despite the gun being pointed at his brother. I was instantly yanked backward. My body was pressed against my captor's large gut and though in the past it wouldn't have bothered me, tonight the feeling repulsed me.

"Okay, you can have her." Malcolm said to the surprise of everyone standing in the alley

We all went quiet. The only sound was of the thunder in the distance. My eyes went wide as did Kenneth's. I looked to Kenneth then to Malcolm.

Malcolm was a son of a bitch! Was he really going to just leave me here?

"What?" Kenneth said turning to his brother.

"Ken just be quiet."

I looked into Malcolm's eyes and I believed him. He was going to let me be taken. He was going to let me end up like all the rest of the women in the club. I knew at that moment I was going to have to save myself. I refused to end up six feet under or lying bloodied and dying somewhere.

"Take Kim. Since you love her so much I know you won't hurt her. Just don't hurt my brother."

I began to wrestle with the man holding me. He put the gun back against my temple. I didn't care. I squirmed and moved trying to break his hold on me. Malcolm and Kenneth were going to leave me and that brought the fight out of me. I was on my own here. I needed to put some distance between me and this killer.

Again, he began to drag me down the alley. This time I could feel his strength. He was determined to get me out of here. I had no clue where he wanted to take me. It didn't matter. My plans rejected that notion. I wasn't going anywhere. I continued to fight him knowing he could shoot me at any moment.

"You can't do that!" Kenneth said.

I didn't know whether Kenneth was talking to me or the man holding the gun.

Both brothers moved closer.

"I can do whatever I want. I have the gun," he reminded them.

He moved the gun away from me and pointed it at Malcolm then at Kenneth. He was erratic and I could tell that with every step they took toward him, it made him more unpredictable.

He could shoot either one of them at a moment's notice.

I couldn't let that happen. I continued to fight trying to elbow him in the ribs and pull my head from the hold he had around my neck. It paid off. His grip loosened and I could tell his focus was on the two men in front of him…and not on me.

I only had a second.

I took one step to the side, raised my fist and with everything I had…punched him as hard as I could.

In the balls.

I landed the blow that would free me and liberate me it did. He immediately grabbed for his aching scrotum and in the process, released me.

I didn't waste the chance I had. I ran. When I heard a loud pop, I ran even faster. I rushed right over to Kenneth and practically jumped into his arms.

"My shoulder…" he reminded me with a grimace.

"I'm so sorry but we have to get out of here."

"We…can't," he said. "Malcolm…"

That was when I finally noticed the fight going on behind me.

Malcolm was in a full on battle with my captor. They were tussling and rolling all over the wet pavement. I knew Kenneth needed medical attention but I couldn't just leave Malcolm there.

"Shit!" Kenneth said before dropping to his knees. I couldn't tell if he was sweating or if his face was wet from the rain that continued to steadily come down. I dropped to my knees in front of him.

"Let me see your shoulder." I said.

He moved his hand. I could tell he was still bleeding profusely.

"You need to take off your shirt."

Together we undid the tie and cautiously he removed his shirt. He was wearing a tank top underneath so he wasn't completely shirtless in the rain. I wrapped his shirt around the wound and pulled it tight.

"Aaaah!" he screamed.

I knew that it hurt but we had to stop the bleeding.

"Kenneth get the gun!" we heard Malcolm yell.

Kenneth was in no place to assist. His eyes were closed and his lips were pursed together trying to hold on through the pain. No. Kenneth wasn't going to be of any help to anyone.

In the meantime, Malcolm was still wrestling with the killer. As they rolled I could see the gleam of the gun in the dim alley light. Malcolm was in the fight of his life and I knew that I couldn't just sit around and do nothing.

I ran toward the fence. I remembered the piece of wood I had seen before. I reached for the broken part of the enclosure that was lying in a puddle of rain water. It was solid and heavy in my hands. I rushed back over to where the two men were fighting.

"Kim, just stay back!" Kenneth called to me.

I ignored his command and headed over to where the two men were struggling. I was determined to stop this before it got worse.

I watched as they rolled back and forth. I needed just the right moment. Just as Malcolm was rolled underneath the other man I swung. I hit Malcolm just as he was rolled back on top.

I tried again and again with not much success. I would occasionally hit Malcolm and then the killer. My attempts seemed to have no affect on the fight.

Then I heard a pop. It was muffled but I knew the sound. It was the third time I had heard it tonight. I felt sick to my stomach.

I dropped the piece of wood and froze. Malcolm was lying on top of the other man. He wasn't stirring. Finally and slowly he rolled off landing next to the man he was just brawling with.

"Malcolm!" Kenneth cried.

We were frozen not sure what to do as they lay side by side not really moving.

Kenneth, still in agony, was the first to stir. He slowly crawled over to his brother. I looked and saw there was blood on both men. I moved over to Malcolm and knelt down next to him. He seemed to be out cold and that terrified me. I began to rip off his shirt looking for a wound that I could put pressure on and hopefully stop the bleeding. When I got to his bare chest I realized...he wasn't shot.

There was no wound.

"Kim...Malcolm?" Kenneth said.

I looked over at him.

"Malcolm's fine," I replied.

That's when I looked over and saw the other man convulsing. His head was turned toward me. I moved over to him and thought about what I should do. He was coughing up blood. I wasn't a doctor but I knew the bullet must have hit his lungs. He seemed to be struggling to breathe. Inside I was panicking. Kenneth was lying on the ground groaning. I had no idea if the bullet that struck him hit a major artery or something.

Everyone around me was either unconscious, in pain or dying. I was in such shock I couldn't move. I was overwhelmed with the scene.

When my captor touched my leg...it reactivated me. I sprung into action pulling my hoodie over my head and placing it on the gushing wound in his chest. I pressed down on it hoping this would help. I knew it wouldn't. His lungs had to be filling up with blood because with every breath took more blood spilled from his mouth.

He was going to die and there wasn't anything anyone could do about it.

His eyes were wide and they spoke to me. They told me he was afraid. He knew he was dying. It was strange.

I began to cry. I had no idea where the tears came from but I began to cry for him.

"Kim," Kenneth called. "Is he…?"

I looked over at him and nodded. He lay back down. A sigh escaped his lips. I brought my attention back to the man below me gasping for breath. He reached out his hand to me.

I hesitated.

Could I comfort the man that killed April? The man that killed so many others? The man that was going to kill me?

I placed my hand in his. We entwined fingers. I tried my best to comfort him in his last few minutes. I leaned down and whispered in his ear. His eyes reacted to my words. They were no longer wide but softened as if he was grateful for my expression of forgiveness.

I had no clue why I held so much sympathy for this man. He was a murderer. A killer. If this bullet hadn't stopped him he would continue to kill. I was sure of it. I was almost one of his victims.

I shouldn't care what happened to him. But I did. I cared an awful lot. He was there for me from day one. He was my confidant and the person I went to when neither April nor Sasha would understand. It was still unreal that he could be so dangerous and sadistic.

My brain made excuses. I thought maybe he was mentally ill. He had to be to do what he did. To slaughter Ashley and April in that fashion. And maybe someone hurt him as a child. Maybe I was crazy for taking pity on him.

No matter what he did…it was done. His reign of terror was over. No more women were going to die.

Deep inside I knew my compassion outweighed my anger. I couldn't explain it but I knew…I wasn't going to let Luciano die alone.

CHAPTER 43

Luciano

"Kenneth, get the gun!" Malcolm yelled.

The gun.

It was my weapon of choice tonight. Not as fulfilling as using my bare hands but when it came down to it…it was quicker and much more effective. I had planned to use it for persuasion. To get Kim to come with me. I didn't intend to use a bullet on anyone.

However, it had since gone off at least twice now.

When Malcolm knocked me down the gun flew out of my hands. I didn't have time to react. Not enough time to find it before I was being pummeled. He landed blow after blow before I was able to smash him across the face with a rock. He fell over and I went to work looking for the gun.

Lightening lit up the night sky and the ground of the alley came into view. We both spotted the gun at the same time. Without hesitation, he went for it. I attempted to possess the handgun as well crawling on my knees, splashing through puddles hoping to get to it first. He was ahead of me crawling, eager to hold the weapon and take control.

I refused to let this be the end. I was going to get the gun, kill this son of a bitch and his brother then have my way with Kim. It was my destiny and he wasn't going to get in the way of it.

I grabbed his ankles and pulled. He landed flat on his face. That gave me the opportunity to go for it. That was when he yelled for Kenneth. It was too late. There would be no time for him to retrieve it before me.

I told myself I would use it on Kenneth immediately. I hated him the most. He wanted to take Kim from me and make her his own. There was no way I was going to let that happen.

Over my dead body.

I reclaimed the gun but before I had a good enough grip on it, Malcolm was on me trying to flip me over. He succeeded in getting me on my back. He was on top trying to pry the gun from my hands. I held on tight refusing to let him win. I wasn't going to lose.

Anger welled up in my chest and spilled throughout my body engulfing me with a rage I had never felt before.

"I'm going to kill you!" I growled surprising myself.

The voice that exited my body didn't sound like my own. In fact none of this was like me. I had never killed before Sarah. Never even thought about it. Yet here I was with numerous murders under my belt and a compelling urge to kill the man on top of me.

My words must have surprised him. His eyes widened and for a second I almost thought he would give up the fight. I was wrong. It only made him more determined to get the weapon.

The rain held us in its folds making it hard to keep my grip on the slippery metal. Malcolm used that to his advantage. He punched me in the jaw again trying to throw me off my game and easing the gun away from me. I landed a blow to his face. It hit him squarely in the nose.

We rolled back and forth. He would be on top and then I would fight and maneuver and end up back on top. It was a battle for power and I was determined to have it. It was almost as satisfying as wrapping my hands around the necks of the women in my possession. The power I would hold over them was intoxicating. And this battle was hitting the same buttons fueling my fire and getting my adrenaline going.

I had to kill him. Just like I did the women.

We continued to wrestle when I was hit in the shoulder by an object. I didn't have any chance to react as the gun almost slipped from my grasp. I reached over with my other hand and punched Malcolm in the face. It gave me only a few seconds of reprieve. Slightly enough time to see that it was Kim swinging a large object in our direction. At her next swing, I rolled us over. Malcolm was hit across the back. It didn't seem to faze him.

The battle continued.

We rolled again. I tried to free myself from his grasp by pushing my hand down. My objective was to shoot him somewhere…anywhere to get him off me. My finger was on the trigger. I tried to squeeze it a couple of times. Before I could fire, he was back on top pulling my wrist, combating my efforts.

We ended up on our sides trying to land more punches. I could not free the gun from between our bodies. They were sandwiched together and no attempts on my part would aid the situation. I was livid by this point. I used my free hand to hit him as many times as I could. If I couldn't shoot him then I would beat him to a bloody pulp.

He dodged some of my attacks and landed a few of his own. The gun was still wedged between us with my hand snugly on the trigger. I yanked. He pulled. We continued this dance with the gun pointing at me and then at him for a couple of minutes.

It felt like an eternity.

Just as a loud rumble of thunder tore through the night, a deafening bang ripped through the air. The impact knocked the wind out of me. I felt pressure on my chest. I assumed it was from the man lying on top of me. He stayed that way for what seemed like forever. When he finally moved, there was no relief.

I coughed up blood.

I had been shot.

The realization sent a shockwave throughout my body. I felt hot and cold all at the same time. Then there was pain. A massive amount of pain.

I heard voices around me but I couldn't speak. I turned my head just enough to see her. To see Kim. She was coming over to me. Her eyes were the size of saucers. She just stared at me as if she were a beautifully sculpted statue. Her expression told me I was in trouble.

I tried to reach out to her. I knew I was losing this battle and I needed her to know.

You have to warn them.

I touched the only part of her that was the least painful to reach. Her leg. Instantly she came to life. She went into action yanking off her sweater and placing it on me. She pressed against the wound and the pain was immeasurable. I wanted to scream out in agony but how can you do that when you could barely breathe?

"Kim, is he…?" I heard Kenneth ask.

I didn't hear her reply. It didn't matter. I already knew the answer.

I reached out my hand to her. I needed something to ground me to this world if only for a few moments. I wasn't sure if she was going to grant this one dying wish but she did tangling her fingers with mine.

She bent down close to my ear and whispered.

"I'm here Luciano. You won't do this alone."

I lay on my back trying to find air that seemed to elude me. My body, from the shock, was involuntarily convulsing and I felt as if I had been kicked in the chest by a horse with branding irons for shoes.

Everything felt intense and surreal.

My life played in my mind like a movie. Childhood. Teen years. Adulthood. My entire life I was always losing. I wasn't good at sports. I never made either of my parents proud. I wasn't good looking and the girls at the lounge wanted nothing to do with me.

Except Kim.

She was always there for me. Even now, holding my hand…comforting me as my soul drained from my body.

You have to warn them.

My thoughts bellowed loudly in my head. There was something I needed to tell her but the more I tried the more blood spurted from my mouth and rendered me useless.

I decided to focus on the pleasure in my life and not my painful past. Nothing was more satisfying then when I had my hands around those beautiful necks or smashed a pillow against Abigail's face. It was truly the highlight of my life. Would I do it all over again?

Yes.

Yes I would.

To feel what I felt I would do it a hundred times.

You have to warn them.

Yes. I needed to warn them. Somehow I needed to let them know. They may have gotten rid of me but this wasn't the end. My death would not terminate the trouble they were all in.

As much as I would like to take credit…I didn't kill Ashley.

Though I would have liked to.

No.

Ashley was the product of pure viciousness and greed.

There was someone else on the hunt and he was not afraid to get bloody.

www.ingramcontent.com/pod-product-compliance
Lightning Source LLC
Chambersburg PA
CBHW031705170626
46808CB00005B/1622